I0520220

The Escape From Heaven

By

Richard A. Woodward

Contents TABLE OF CONTENTS

PART I

The Retelling

"After Wormwood struck Earth in late 2021, the human race came close to extinction, and society and history had come to an end," a little girl of nine says, addressing a crowded school hall filled with her peers, friends, teachers and their families. "To rebuild the human race, the survivors of the Impact had only their memories and bits and pieces of some artifacts from the now-extinct society.

"Life was near impossible, and it only got worse when Satan saw the humans' souls at their weakest, their morale broken. Most were desperate for answers and relief; Satan took full advantage, trying to take over their shattered world completely by assimilating himself as a powerful leader.

"For years, he tricked the suffering humans by offering peace, unity, and wealth for everyone. Most followed the rule of this diabolical leader, not knowing that their wealth and prosperity would come at the greatest price: the forfeit of their souls. Those that didn't join were hunted down. Anyone caught was immediately tortured to expose the locations of others in hiding, and if they didn't give up that information, they were killed.

"All those that were successful in remaining hidden throughout the world prayed for help, only to have their prayers go unanswered." The little girl with auburn hair down below her shoulders went on telling her story to a captive audience, who listened to her words and watched projections of her descriptions being displayed throughout the auditorium.

"For years, this was the fate of the human species, with Satan collecting more and more souls to build up an army for his own personal war against God. While most followed under fear for their lives, some seemed to enjoy inflicting pain on the people that were caught." The audience groaned in disgust. "It seemed all that was ever good on Earth and in the human soul was to be lost, forever." Cries erupted from some of the younger children, and their parents tried to calm them down so the rest of the story could be told. The young girl behind the lectern smiled, continuing.

"However, as it was foretold a millennium before, Satan would try, and fail. God saved us. He came back to Earth, where the Great Battle of Souls took place, and put a stop to Satan's supremacy. He restored order, love, and resurrected the human spirit that had seemed all but doomed to fall victim to the subtle, mysteriously dark and alluring ways of evil that were plaguing the world.

"Not everything survived the tumultuous times of the Impact and subsequent Apocalypse. The Great Battle of Souls between God and Satan had taken its toll. Billions of people had died, and a countless number of other species had also perished from the devastation. Humankind had never experienced such hardship before and hoped never to again.

"What was once called 'The City of Brotherly Love' is now called the city of Aeon, this city, is where the final battle between God and Satan took place and where evil was vanquished. Satan's powers were stripped and he was imprisoned for the rest of eternity inside an electrified force field called the Cage of Satan. Humiliated from defeat and trapped inside this cage, Satan, in hopes of saving some pride in himself, changed his appearance from that of the once-powerful world leader that had humanity on its knees into a luminescent mist known as the Pother of Satan." A thick, choking fog started filling up the room, glowing dully, changing colors. The whole auditorium full of people started to murmur, growing anxious; again the younger children cried out with fright and uncertainty.

She carried on telling her story. "He was put on display for all of us as a reminder that we are loved by God, and that Satan's horrors and the unimaginable evil that lies within all of us even to this day, were securely locked away in the Cage of Satan. Although his powers cannot reach outside the electrified field, he changes his appearance from the Pother into an onlooker's most beloved thing in the world, luring them to go *inside* the Cage so he can escape through their bodies to walk in the outside world once again. A warning was given to us to never stare at the Pother of Satan for any longer than a few seconds. In doing so, we would allow his powers to seep into us, driving us mad beyond anything we could ever imagine. Once among us, Satan's powers would only spread like a virus from there, growing stronger with each person he infects. Finding our weaknesses and using them against us, he would start an unstoppable chain reaction that would let loose his full realm of powers upon us, leaving humankind to once again suffer his scornful wrath." One child started screaming loudly and had to be removed from the hall by his mother.

"However, because Satan was defeated, there was a new future possible for the human race, one of love, happiness, and prosperity for all. For God was among us." The whole place erupted in excitement. "After the Great Battle of Souls, God worked with the survivors, called the Old, in the creation of a new human species: the Modified-Sapiens, or the Modiens. Us. For nearly a thousand years, God lived among us and helped us become better beings. Beings of great intelligence, beings that far surpass anything He had created before." More cheers filled the hall. "The Old and the Modiens were to rebuild the human race and establish a new history on the Earth, which was given back to the Old as a reward for their suffering, a New Earth on which the new species could grow and prosper. And prosper we have!" The crowd cheered again, everyone clapping and standing on their feet in acknowledgement of their Creator and for the achievements they have accomplished.

"Then, after 999 years, God felt that we were capable of living on our own, and, with hopes that we would live on as yet another wonderful creation of His, He left. We shall not mourn His departure. Rather we will embrace the extraordinary lives that He has given us. We shall have a new history, a history filled with exploration not just of ourselves but also of our entire universe! We are free to explore our vast universe without fear, pain, or even death, as anyone has known it before. We are free to choose our own path and show to the universe what we are capable of doing. All that might stop us is the choices we have to make from now on to determine what is best for our future. I leave you with this question: What do you think we should do with the glorious existence given us by God?"

The young girl bowed her head, acknowledging that she had finished. Everyone stood up and cheered with delight for the valedictorian of the Nine-Year-Old Class of Aeon and her powerful speech. "Thank you, thank you. This moment means a lot to me; you have no idea how this feels right now. Father, where are you?" She looked around at the thousands of faces looking up at her.

"He's right here! Stand up, buddy! Don't think you can hide behind your modesty now! Your daughter is looking for you."

A reluctant Michael, embarrassed, just laughed as he pushed away his best friends' arms. He stood, and waved to the boisterous crowd. "Now, now, everyone. This night isn't about me, it's about these kids. Let's hear it for them." The crowd grew louder still as they turned their applause back to the young girl and the rest of the class she was standing in front of. The crowd went silent, waiting for her to speak again.

"I'd just like to say a few last things. Daddy, I wouldn't be here if it wasn't for your guidance and patience with me," she snickered, and then composed herself again. "This man here has influenced me so much in my life, he has taught me more than I could ever dream of, and I'd like to thank him from the bottom of my heart. But, it wasn't just him; my mother has also helped me throughout these years. Thank you, Mom. And, it was more than just my parents who molded me into who I am now; it was all of you. Without my teachers, friends, and loved ones, I wouldn't be the person that I am now. Who knows where I would be without all of you? Everyone here has taught me something about life in his or her own way. Thank you, everyone; you are all a piece of me, forever. With all this knowledge you have given me, I feel I know what life is really about: Helping others grow to be a better being. And how does someone help another grow? By teaching them what you have learned, sharing that knowledge with as many as you can and helping others grow as individuals. I love the knowledge that's been shared with me in my short nine years. It makes me want to learn even more, and I can only appreciate your thirst for it with the experience most of you have within you here tonight. I see a new future, one that will have us Modiens learning new things for thousands of years to come, if not forever." The crowd shouted out again with a thunderous cheer.

"I feel by the time I'm done tonight, you will have a new view upon life itself, and of things to come. You will scale the depths of knowledge to find who you are, and what makes our kind what it is. Together we will rain upon others our wonderful new thoughts and make others tremble in fear of our knowledge of what is right, and what is the way of the Modien life." Another round of cheering from the audience filled the auditorium.

"A wonderful, caring, and very smart woman once said, 'With the new day comes new strength and new thoughts.' Today, I feel, is that new day. And I only pray you find new strength for all these new thoughts you are about to experience."

With that, she raised her hands out, and thousands of her nano-bots streamed out from her fingertips in all directions, racing toward her people. The audience started shrieking in horror as some were struck with a terrific force, ripping chunks out of their bodies, sparks spraying from their wounds. Dozens died instantly and countless more were wounded, strewn across the floor. The former mood of harmony was utterly destroyed in an instant; pandemonium reigned now, everyone running for the nearest exit in sheer terror.

Michael screamed, pushing panicking people aside, "Amanda! No!"

"It's too late now, Father, and this is only the beginning." She smiled. "But don't worry, Father, I won't hurt you or Mom."

Michael saw his daughter walking toward him. He closed his eyes and opened them again to see nothing at all, no auditorium, and no screaming people running around in fear. Nothing.

A Glimpse of Society

"Daddy, Daddy! Are you okay? Are you daydreaming again?" The young girl in his day dreams watched on uncertainly. "Daddy, snap out of it! You're scaring me. I was asking you what you thought my speech should be about and you just stood there with this frightened look on your face."

"What?" He blinked his brown, water-filled eyes a couple of times. "Oh, yes. Sorry darling, I guess I was daydreaming again." He realized that he was in his home and not actually in that horrendous scene of death and destruction. Michael let out a sigh of relief. "What were you asking again?"

"Daddy," she began, frustrated, "you promised you'd help me with my valedictorian speech. What should I say? I've never given one of these before. What did you say when you had to give one?"

"Well, Amanda angel, the only thing I can really say is to speak from the heart. Say what you think is right, and how you feel. This is going to be *your* night, after all. I want you to dig deep inside you and express what you're feeling from within. Other than that, I don't want to put words in your mouth or thoughts in your head. You're your own person with your own ideas and dreams. I don't want to stifle that."

She smiled widely, giving him a hug. "Awww, Daddy, you always say just the right thing. I'ma go and get started on it right now."

"You do that, angel."

She let out a short shout of excitement and ran off to her room.

Michael sighed again in relief that he was only daydreaming, but he was confused as to where those thoughts had come from and why they were so violent. "Who knows? It's probably nothing," he thought. He called over the Flying Food Fabricator. "Are you hungry, Amanda?"

"Always, Daddy!"

"How about some bacon and eggs?"

"Sounds awesome!"

He put his hand into the sensor of the FFF. A few whirs, beeps, and lights went off and within a couple of seconds, eggs, sunny-side up, along with some strips of bacon, materialized out of the opening.

"Mmmmm, smells great. Amanda, it's ready. Come and get it." He'd started on a slice of bacon when he got a message from his wife. Putting the slice down, he closed his eyes and an image of his wife appeared in his mind's eye. "Hey, sweetheart. How did your meeting go with The High Coalition of Space-Traveling Beings? Did you get your dream job?

"Oh, Michael, the competition to become a diplomat for the T.H.C.S.B. is amazing. There are so many other qualified people to be a representative for our species! It's not fair that each one who applies can't become a diplomat, but I guess that's how things work."

"I can imagine all the others that applied are some pretty extraordinary people. So, did you get the job?"

"Well, the thing is, being a diplomat, one must sometimes have to be gone for long periods of time, sometimes months…."

"Yes, I know. But you still haven't answered me, silly. Were you chosen?"

"That's just the thing…. Where's Amanda? Can you get her, please? I guess she turned off her Modien Messaging System, because I tried contacting her when I called you, but I was told she was unreachable."

"Yeah, she's trying to work on her speech. Hold on, I'll get her." Michael walked out of the kitchen and through the family room to the hall and called out for her. "Amanda, stop what you're doing for a minute. Your mom has to ask us something. Turn on your M.M.S., please."

"What, Daddy? Hang on, let me turn off my music." She closed her blue eyes, those extraordinary eyes that turned gray when she was excited about something, and thought for the stereo system to lower the volume. In the same instant, her thoughts turned on her M.M.S. and a picture of her mother and father appeared. "Okay, there. Mom, are you there? Sorry, I was trying to write my speech and listening to some music. This one song by Clutch, The Soapmakers, it's one of the new songs discovered in a recent excavation. The group writes this song about a time even farther back in history, about these people that were wondering about the future. Just makes me wonder about our future." She shook her head. "Sorry! Mom, are you here?"

"Yes, sweetie, I am. You're so cute sometimes. And to answer your question, Michael, yes, I did get offered a spot, but I wanted to ask you both something."

"What is it, Mommy? I'm trying to write my speech and I just got into a groove."

"Amanda," Michael interjected, "your mother was just awarded a very prestigious position; you should say something nice."

"Sorry, Mom. I guess I don't fully understand is all. It sounds amazing, though. Congratulations!"

Marilyn laughed. "It's okay, baby. Well, sweetie, Mommy has been offered a new job, one that might take her away from the both of you for quite some time. I might be gone for many months sometimes. Do you think that you can handle it?"

"I don't know about Daddy, but I can deal with that. After all, I'm going to be 10 next year, *and* I am valedictorian *this year,*" she said, with a bit of confidence.

"Yes, I know, darling, I'm so proud of you, too. I've always had this feeling you have this special something inside you, ever since you were born. You're really turning into quite a remarkable young woman."

"Awww, Mom, I wish you were here now. I'd give you a huge hug and tell you how proud *I* am of *you.*"

"I wish I was there, too, angel. I could use one of your hugs. Okay. So, Amanda is on board. Now, is that something you can deal with, Michael? I don't know when I'd start, but I'm guessing as soon as I accept." Marilyn let out a sigh. "I *do* know I will miss you and Amanda dearly, but this is something I feel I just have to do."

"I'll miss you, too, but I can understand that. And if it's something you feel you have to do then who am I to stop you? I'm just so happy to be your husband. You're everything I could have dreamt of in my life."

"You're such an angel; I wouldn't even be here without you. They said they'd let me know when and where my first outpost will be within a couple of days if I accepted. Although there are rumors there's a position free in the Andromeda galaxy."

"Wow, Mom! You're going to the Andromeda galaxy? That's so cool! Can I put that in my speech?"

"Oh my! No, dear," Marilyn laughed nervously, blinking her hazel grey eyes. "Don't mention any of this to anyone; they haven't officially said I have the job yet because I had to ask you two if it was okay."

"Awww … all right, Mommy, but if you do get it, I want to go there with you some time!"

"Okay, angel…. Are you sure you're okay with me leaving for several months at a time? You won't miss me?"

"I always miss you when we're not together, Mommy, but this has been a dream of yours for as long as I can remember, and you should go. Besides, Daddy and I will be fine. Won't we, Daddy?"

"Of course we will, darling. There's nothing we can't accomplish together. Okay, you can go back to writing your speech now if you want, sweetie. I'd like to talk to Mommy alone before she has to go back to work."

"All right, Daddy. I love you, Mommy. Congratulations again on getting your new job!"

"Thank you, angel, I'll see you soon. I love you, too."

With that, Amanda turned off her Modien Messaging System, grabbed a plate of food, and ran off to her room to once again write her speech.

Michael sat back down at the kitchen table and started eating the slice of bacon he had put down before. "So, how's Titan? Is it almost ready for animals to live there now?"

"We got our first DNA shipment of animals yesterday, a bunch of insects, more of them than anything else, actually. We also got some birds and snakes, some rodents. The rest will come once we grow this first shipment. However, I'm going to assign someone to that. I miss you guys and I feel it's time for me to come home before I start this new assignment."

"Well, I miss you, too. That's incredible news, though. How many planets and moons in our solar system have you terra-formed now, six?"

"Yeah, this is my sixth," Marilyn answered, with awe at her accomplishments. "I'm very lucky I got this one, even. There aren't many places left in our solar system to transform. I wonder if T.H.C.S.B. will ever lift that ban they initiated after the Mysorians completely killed off the Vrillians. I mean, hasn't it been over 300 years since that happened?"

"Yeah. Wow, it seems like it was just yesterday when I heard about that. I remember asking my dad why anyone would do such a thing, and he said some people just don't understand the value of life."

"That's so sad. The Mysorians always seem to figure out a way around the laws to scorch a path of destruction across the universe. They are pure evil, if I ever saw or heard of evil before. I still don't understand how the Coalition hasn't figured out a way to deal with the Mysorians' actions, though. I mean, since they've killed the Vrillians, they have colonized countless other solar systems without authorization, even after joining the Coalition. The horror they spew upon others just before they kill them, it's unspeakable. I just don't get it. I don't get how they could have been allowed into T.H.C.S.B. to begin with, especially after murdering the Vrillians."

"I don't get that either; it is very worrisome. Something has to be done, for sure. The scary part is that no one knows what the Mysorians even look like. The fact that most of the Mysorians themselves don't even know what the species actually looks like is simply amazing, to say the least. As far as I know, the Mysorians have been around since the beginning of time, and the records of their origins have been destroyed. It was weird when they joined the Coalition and assimilated themselves as very tall and blonde-haired. Although many say that that still isn't their true identity. I still wonder what they could look like." Michael shuddered uncontrollably. "I get this feeling something horrible is going to happen soon."

"What do you mean?"

"I don't know. You know how I get these feelings sometimes. This one is different, though, it's...." He hesitated and started cutting up some the egg with his fork while looking for the right words. "It's not like any of the other feelings I've had before when something good would happen. Like when I had that feeling just before you just found out you'd be working on terra-forming Titan."

"What do you think it is, then?"

"I can't explain it, but something is off. Something doesn't feel right. I saw images of people screaming and running away in terror at Amanda's ceremony."

"Awww, baby. Everything will be fine. You're probably just feeling anxious on her behalf. Besides, you're not the only one who gets those feelings," Marilyn reassured her husband.

"You're probably right; you always are." Michael sighed in relief. "So, you're coming home soon, then?"

"Uh huh, I'll get Crystal to do the rest of the work here. She's wanted to do more lately since she broke up with her last boyfriend. I feel sorry for her. She's had so many boyfriends. She can't seem to find that special someone. And it's not because she's unattractive. I mean, she is a smart, tall, blonde.... I know you guys like that type."

"Well, not everyone can be as lucky as we were. And not all guys like blondes; if that were true, we'd never have met."

Marilyn giggled. "That's true. I wish she'd like Christopher, though. I think they'd make a great couple. He reminds me a lot of you, always trying to make everyone smile and feel good, and he was shy at first when I hired him, just like when I first met you. Only he has blonde hair, too, and, fortunately for you, I'm, not attracted to blondes, either. But Crystal and Chris just can't seem to find that connection."

"You know what they say, 'love is blind.'"

"So true. Anyway, I should go. I have to tell Crystal that I'm leaving and that I trust her to get the job done; hopefully that will boost her confidence some. I think I'll have Christopher stay behind, too, and help her out," Marilyn smiled, enjoying playing matchmaker.

"Okay, baby. Do you want me to meet you at the teleport?"

"No, it's okay. I was going to do something special for dinner for us before I got home anyway, and I have to make the arrangements. I'll be home afterward, though."

"Wow, you *do* miss us," exclaimed Michael. "What could it be that the Flying Food Fabricator or any other restaurant couldn't make for us?"

"Well, it's either—"

"I'm sorry, Marilyn. I don't mean to interrupt, I heard you talking. Are you talking to Michael?" Crystal said as she burst into the room. She carried on without waiting for an answer. "I think I found a more efficient way to speed up the process of implementing the insects and rodents on Titan so we can move on with the bigger animals sooner. It should save a good 18 hours."

"Eighteen hours? That's amazing! That's why I hired you, Crystal—you're so good at math. That's far beyond what I could calculate. You're just like Christopher," Marilyn said. "In fact, the two of you will finish Titan. I think you're ready for this step now."

Crystal smiled. "You really think so? I thought I was, but I didn't want to say anything. I mean, with your accomplishments, I was sure you had to think I was ready by now, but I just wasn't sure you thought that for sure.… Oh my,

I'm repeating myself, forgive me. Thank you, though! This is such an amazing feeling. Does Christopher know yet?"

Marilyn smiled and hugged her friend and mentee. "Nope, not yet. You can tell him if you want. Just pick the right people to help you, but you know that already; you'll do fine. And tell him bye for me. I'll see him when I get back. Congrats, and tell Christopher that I'm sorry I didn't tell him in person, but I miss my family."

"Okay, Boss."

Marilyn burst out laughing. "How many times have I told you not to call me that?"

"You want the actual number, or…?"

Marilyn laughed again. "You see how funny you can be? You just have to open up more. You will meet someone, you'll see, and he will be perfect. I just know it, I can feel it."

Crystal shrugged. "I sure hope so; it's been so long. I want to meet 'Mr. Right' already and have kids," she sighed.

"Hey, now, none of that. I promise you that you will meet him soon. Just keep your chin up. You never know, he could be right in front of you just waiting to be noticed."

"Thanks, Marilyn; you're such a good friend. Now go home and enjoy your perfect life," Crystal said with a slight undertone of jealousy, which was picked up neither by Marilyn nor Michael, who was waiting patiently. "I'll be fine; I always am."

"Yes, you will be, and soon with Mr. Right, you just wait. Never give up hope." Marilyn gave Crystal another hug and watched her walk out the room, calling out Christopher's name, and turned her attention back to her husband. "Sorry about that, honey! Now, where were we? Oh, yes, where we are eating tonight. Any guesses?"

"Hmmm, is it what I'm thinking? We haven't been there in a while."

"Hmmm, could be, you'll just have to wait and find out," Marilyn replied with a grin on her face.

"Well, I can't wait to see you nonetheless. I should get going; it's time for Amanda to go to school, and I gotta get to work. I love you."

"I love you, too. Tell Amanda bye for me but don't tell her about dinner. I want to surprise her."

"Okay, angel. Be safe."

"Thanks. You, too."

They both turn off each other's signals telepathically. Michael touched another slice of bacon and it was absorbed through his fingertips. "Mmmmm, just how I like it. Crispy, but not *too* crispy." He finishes the rest of his breakfast by swiping his hand over it, the food micro-absorbed into his body like the bacon. "Amanda, it's time for school, angel. You can work on your speech later."

Running out of her room, she said, "Awww, okay. I was just getting on a roll, too. I found this really great quote I want to use. This woman that was called a "first lady" said it. She had lots of interesting sayings, but there was this one in particular that I liked the best. I found it most relevant to my speech."

"That's wonderful, dear, but we have to hurry before we're late."

"All right, Daddy. I'm ready." She grabbed his hand and they both walked out the door and into the air tube, which whisked them up to the roof by sending a powerful air current over their bodies, slightly separating their trillions of nano-bots. As they stepped out of the tube, Amanda asked, "Daddy, where do thoughts come from?"

Michael smiled. "Oh, baby, if I only had an answer for that. People have been asking that question since the dawn of time. It's just one of those things in life that can't be answered. The Old even asked that question of God once after he saved them."

"Wow! What'd He say?"

"He said, 'That's a very good question, let me get back to you after I think about that.'"

Amanda just looked at him and blinked a couple of times. "Is that it?"

"Yeah, not very satisfying, is it? However, it's sort of funny to me. What made you ask that?"

"I don't know, that's why I was asking," she exclaimed.

Michael burst out in laughter as they reached the edge of the roof and looked down at the city. "Fair enough, angel. Come on, you ready?"

"You bet. I love this part!" She took his hand again and they backed away from the edge of the building, ran forward at full speed, and jumped off. They both spread their arms out and shouted with glee as they started soaring down to the ground, miles below them.

Looking out over the city of Aeon as he glided toward the earth, Michael had another vision. As he looked over at his daughter sailing next to him, he saw the scenery start to change all around her. Within a few seconds, the view changed from massive skyscrapers, and cars soaring through the air and trees, to a thick jungle and a stone building enveloping both of them. There was a brief moment of darkness. "What, what's going on here?" Michael said out loud. "Why can't I move?"

"Awww, Daddy. That's because we don't want you to move, silly. Don't worry, though, you'll be okay. As long as you *don't* move, that is." Amanda giggled. Still dazed, he heard her speak again. His vision focused and he saw her standing next to his father. "Now, Daddy, I hope you do realize that this wasn't part of *my* plan; *I* had no control over this part. But I do want you to know I love you so much, and hope you'll soon realize why we're doing all this."

"Now, Amanda, darling, let your father readjust himself. I don't think he realizes what exactly it is he's been through."

"Okay, Grandpa. Can I play with my new toys now, please?"

"Sure, angel. Run along now, I'll call you if need be."

Michael couldn't believe his eyes. He saw his father, who'd passed on almost 200 years before, yet he couldn't imagine how or when he could have gone to the Building of Souls and gone into the Machine of Forever. "Dad," he said, "what's happening? Why am I here?"

"Why are you here? I'll tell you why you're here, my son. You're here to be offered the chance of a lifetime, of all lifetimes."

Michael looked around and, still dazed, he realized he still couldn't move and that he was strapped into some sort of chair.

"You don't get it, do you, Michael?"

"Apparently not, Father. Please, tell me what I'm missing."

"Do you know how I know that "God" isn't God? You might be thinking it's just a hunch, or a guess, or an assumption, but it's not."

"So, what is it then Dad?"

"He told me. Simple as that."

"He told you?"

"Yes."

"What, did He just come out and say it one night at dinner or something?"

"Well, actually, yes. He told me many things that night, just before I passed on. Actually, I don't know why He waited until then to tell me."

"Does anyone else know?"

"Beats me. I think some members of the Old know, though. I might have heard some talk about it for a little bit, then I heard nothing all of a sudden, because, you know, I died," he said, the anger and resentment strong in his voice.

"So what exactly did he say, then? I'm curious."

"Well, since I think you won't figure out a way to escape from here, I *will* tell you. You should feel grateful, Michael. Privileged, even."

"Yeah, yeah. I'm honored and will forever be in your debt for this knowledge," Michael said acerbically.

"I'll forget I heard such rudeness. You don't get it, Michael, this information will change human history forever, and I will reap in the benefits. Now, you either, can join me and your daughter and be in on the ground floor, or you can sit here and rot, for all I care. Sorry for being so blunt, but I'm sick of being in this primitive society. It's of no use to me anymore, and I am rather looking forward to being on the outside once again."

"So, go on and tell me. Tell me this powerful bit of information that will 'change human history.'"

His father's eyes grow wide with rage and he slapped his son across the head, making Michael move. An arc of electricity sparked between Michael's head and his father's hand. His father just laughed, ignoring the pain soaring through his arm.

Before passing out, Michael found the strength to utter, "Why are you doing this?"

He barely understood his father's response. "I'll tell you later, but right now, watch out for the ground."

Michael heard Amanda's voice once again. "What, Daddy?" she asked, without noticing the frightened look on her father's face, "Why am I doing what? We're just going to the car like usual, remember? Were you daydreaming again? Better snap out of it; we're close to landing, silly."

Coming to his senses, Michael looked down and saw the ground rushing closer and closer to him. He positioned himself and landed perfectly, as usual. "Wow, that was a weird daydream."

"How so, Daddy?"

"I don't know; it was so strange. I saw my father, and you were there." He explained what he saw as they walked to his car. "I don't know how I got there, but I remember I couldn't move. It was so weird."

"Huh. Wow, Daddy. That *is* strange. Are you okay?"

"Yeah, I just have to shake it off, I guess. It just seemed so real. Oh well, I just hope I don't have any others like it ever again." Michael opened the door to his classic 1967 Pontiac GTO.

"Why is that, Daddy?" Amanda asked. Michael climbed into his car and closed the door behind him, then just sat there as though remembering the vision. "Daddy, you're really starting to scare me now! What's going on that you're not telling me?"

"Awww, angel, they're just daydreams, nothing more. I'll be fine, I promise," Michael reassured her as he turned on the car. He gave the old goat a voice command to head to Amanda's school.

"Are you sure, Daddy? I mean, I heard some people that have weird and scary daydreams are really being taken over by Satan. I heard that's what happened to those two people that were taken away from the Pother recently."

Stunned, Michael blurted out, "How do you know any of that? *I* haven't even heard the details as to what happened to them."

"Hahaha, I had you going, Daddy! How would I know what happened to them? That is sad, though, I mean, if it's true. I wouldn't know what to do without you, you going crazy and all," she teased.

"Very funny," he answered, laughing along with her. "You had me going there for a second, you and that vivid imagination of yours." Michael rubbed his hand over her head. "You're such a trickster. Reminds me of your mother."

"Wow, really? Mom? You're talking about *my* mom? Are you sure?" Amanda asked as she slid out the food tray from the door panel and put her thumb on the sensor. Out sprang a B.L.T.

"Hungry again? I forget how much we eat as we're growing up. And yes, your mom is very funny when you get her going."

"Wow, I never would have guessed. How come I've never seen her be funny? I'm going to be ten next year and all I've seen her do is laugh at your jokes and sometimes mine."

"Hard to believe, isn't it? I don't know what's happened to her funny side recently. When you were real young, she used to make you laugh and giggle all the time. She's been more involved in her work lately. But trust me, she can be hilarious."

"Tell me something she did that was funny. Please?"

As Michael told stories about Marilyn, his car soared through the air of the mega city of Aeon along the skyways of cars that layered and crisscrossed through the immense buildings. Skyscrapers as high as the eye could see stretched miles into the sky, the city stretching out hundreds of miles in all directions. Aeon was one of the biggest cities on the New Earth, one of a hundred cities spread throughout the world, each holding a maximum of 10 million people. The huge cities of the New Earth allowed for the rest of the land to be used in other ways, for amusement or agriculture, with the majority of the land left for nature and all its animals.

They continued their conversation until the car let them know they were almost at their destination. "Wow, that's so funny. How come I never heard any of that before, Daddy?"

"I'm sorry, sweetie. I thought I told you. Hey, you should try to get her to tell you a joke. See what she does."

"Really?"

"Sure, why not? I'd love to see her in that state of mind again. I've tried to get her to laugh lately, but she's just so into her work."

"I know, Daddy. She isn't the same lately, I can even see that. But I'll try that. Sounds fun." She kissed her fathers' head, jumped out the door, and started gliding down to the landing area of her school. "Bye, Daddy! I love you," she screamed. Waving, she fell to earth.

Michael told the car to drive to his job. It started flying off to the Atomic Transference Machine Square in downtown Aeon. After landing in the parking lot, Michael got out of his car and headed off the edge of the building, again soaring down to ground level, and off to start another day at work.

While walking to his office, Michael saw a man screaming, "No! I must save it, she needs me! She needs me!" This man thought he had seen his daughter inside the electrified Cage of Satan, but to all appearances, there was only a mist in the cage The Pother of Satan. For nearly a thousand years, the people have just walked by, seeing Satan caged up in the form of this fog and not thinking twice about it.   This was just the way of life for the Modiens.

Michael read the inscription written on the statue above the electrified cage. "This *is* Evil, this was the FEAR of all. This is 'The One' that has to be here."

A woman next to him confessed nervously, "Oh my, that poor man. I wonder what he saw that made him want to try and get in there so badly."

     "He must have looked at the Pother too long," Michael said to the woman, as more guards rushed to try to subdue the man. "He's the third person this month I've seen that has looked at the Pother too long. I wonder why they're forgetting?" he added.

Just as she was about to answer, one guard pulled out a wand and touched the man's head with the end of it, emitting a deep purple light and creating the Halo of Ataraxia, which knocked the man unconscious. A doorway instantly appeared next to them, and a couple of guards dragged the unconscious man away through it quickly. Once they'd pulled the man through, they all vanished into thin air, doorway included.

"There's nothing to see here, people. This man has just caught a virus which made him forget to not look at the Pother for more than a few seconds. It made him hallucinate. Don't worry, he's going to get the care and attention he deserves and will be fine in a couple of hours."

A few murmurs wandered through the crowd, people wondering what the virus could be. But everyone began to go about their way, laughing and sharing stories or enjoying the day at shops and cafes under perfect weather. Once the guard saw everyone had accepted his explanation, he looked over at the cage quickly, wincing and shaking his head. He walked through a newly appeared doorway and vanished.

"Well, that certainly was odd," the woman declared to Michael. "Anyway, have a nice day, my child. I must complete some remaining preparations before my time comes to pass on."

"Oh my! That's wonderful. Congratulations."

The woman sighed and then answered in a curious tone, "Thank you. Although I love my life and all the things I've done in it, I can't help but wonder what is next for me. I mean, us." She laughed slightly. "I mean, the ones who are going to pass on this cycle. I feel like I've accomplished so much in my life, but I feel something is missing. Maybe I'm just nervous of the unknown."

Michael also paused to think of what may come when he too would pass on. "I always smile when I think of it; my father tells me it's beyond anything he could have imagined, and that there's nothing to worry about, and he was..."

But before Michael could finish, the woman realized who he was and smiled in delight. "Michael? Oh my goodness, it's such an honor to meet you! *I* had no idea. Please forgive me!"

Michael laughed and put his hand on her shoulder. "No worries; there are a lot of people here in Aeon, and with what just happened, I can't blame you for not noticing. But please, act as though I'm just another person, like you. After all, I am. Just because I am the son of Daniel, doesn't mean I'm any different from you."

"You're so humble, Michael. You *are* different, though; you're one in a billion. I thought how after your father acted...." She hesitated so as to not say anything disrespectful of Daniel. "It's just that he was so outgoing and talkative. He was also one in a billion, before there were a billion of us, before any of us. Well, I shall do as you wish, young and benevolent Michael, son of Daniel, the First. I wish you well, my child." With that, she walked off into the dispersing crowd. Michael continued his walk to work.

"To inspire a Homo sapiens, is knowing how to live life to the fullest," was the inscription on top of the entrance to this particular T.A.T.M.S where Michael worked. He thought it was a little lame, to be honest, but that was a quote from God, so it made him smile and try to do his best to inspire all of his Homo sapiens every day.

Michael entered the hallway of this T.A.T.M.S. and told the security bot who he was, and the bot scanned Michael's Modien Essence Transmitter and clarified that Michael was allowed inside the building and lowered the force shield. He walked over to one of the air tubes that delivered the workers to their floor, stepped inside and was immediately whooshed up miles into the air. "I wonder if the new floors are done today," Michael thought to himself as he watched the view while he ascended, winding through the building.

Each tube had a different path that either wound through the building or ran along the outside of it, or both. It just depended on the random assignment of the computer when the Modiens entered the tubes.

The Modiens loved art and found any possible way to express it with different versions and mediums that they came up with, and each week a Modien won a raffle to determine who got to decorate the rooms the tubes passed through. Usually, the Modiens that worked above one another got together to come up with a certain theme. Since the people that saw the rooms passed by so quickly, they were often decorated almost like a moving scene that worked its way through the building. Michael was amazed at some of the scenes that his fellow workers had come up with in the past. He once saw a stunning display of the asteroids that destroyed the dinosaurs and nearly wiped humanity off the face of the earth. He had never seen such detail put into anything before. He could almost feel the heat of the impacts as they raced toward him.

After passing the first few floors of foundation and hardware of the building, Michael started to fill with excitement to see if the art for this period was done or not. "Almost there! Awww, rats! It's the tube that leads to the skyline view of the city. Oh, well. Gives me time to enjoy the simple things in life, I guess." He finally reached his floor and hopped out of the air tube with ease. Entering the break room, Michael didn't see Gabriel. He must have the day off.

After not seeing his best friend, Michael went about his usual routine of talking to the rest of his friends and co-workers while making his favorite breakfast: S'mores and cappuccino. He had a thing for antiquities. It actually took longer to get to work and do all those things than to do his job. He made some small talk with the rest of his friends while finishing his breakfast and told everyone to have a nice day. He walked off to the room where his A.T.M. was and entered. There was a small desk with a chair attached to it; in the front of the desk there was a tube that connected the desk to the outside of the room through the ceiling. He inserted his Sphere of Life, which had come through his body and detached from the top of his MET, into the tube's opening. It immediately shot up through the tube, out of the room, and out of sight. "Computer, load my universe," Michael demanded. The entire room went completely dark.

A tiny green speck of light suddenly appeared in front of him. A bright flash went off, and he felt a rush of energy jolt through him. "Wooooooo, I love that!" The green speck started expanding, and soon after brilliant points of blue lights appeared to dot the space around him as far as he could see.

"Here they come! I've almost lost track of how many stars I have in my universe."

A voice came out of the darkness, answering Michael's wonderment. "The number of stars you have in numeric value is 420,681,942,087,215,346,773, the number of planets 314, 1."

"Thank you, computer, I was just being…. Never mind, you won't understand. Computer, load up the last day I was on the planet Amosulemat." Michael watched as his universe started expanding out in every direction and alongside the stars that had just formed; planets started spinning around some of them, and then they all raced off into the distance. "And there they all go, too! I love seeing this part, makes me feel so alive," he muttered. Instantly, he started soaring halfway across his universe. A few seconds later, he saw the planet of Amosulemat growing bigger and bigger beneath his feet. "Computer, land me just outside any major city, please." He started flying through the atmosphere of the planet while being protected by the walls of the actual room he was in, and he descended just outside a city with many skyscrapers and millions of people. As he left the room, he took in a deep breath. "Ahhh, I have to give these people clean-fuel technology someday soon. I keep forgetting how awful fossil fuels smell. I should do that soon while they are still in their technological infancy. "

Being a Modien is hard work sometimes, even in Paradise, and today was no different. Michael was out of ideas and still had one civilization left. He had to have at least one invention for each civilization a Modien worked on … otherwise the planet was lost, recycled into the building blocks for other Modiens to use. That was part of the deal with God and Modiens, although not many planets were lost, since Modiens loved taking care of their Sapiens-Old.

Michael had always been happy soaring through the vast empty spaces of his universe, or buzzing around in one of the busy urban cities on a weekday. He enjoyed his job and all the different ways he could give some Sapiens-Old the inspiration for an invention. However, since he was stumped as to what invention to give this last civilization, and not wanting to give it one that he'd used already today, he decided to go into the jungle on that planet to clear his mind and come up with something new.

He loved the jungle for inspiration for some reason; once, he'd inspired someone to invent the *La-Z-Boy* when he was being chased by a tiger: "What could be better than to be home with my feet up on a comfortable, cushioned chair, instead of being chased by a tiger?" Yet this last planet's invention was eluding his imagination so far. Maybe he was thinking too much. Modiens sometimes did that with all the information they had stored. It takes some time to go through it all, even with their processing speed.

While slashing through the brush, he started noticing patterns, like letters. His mind projected these patterns onto the jungle floor in what looked like words. The motions of the knife he swung, arcing through the brush, reminded him of the arms of typewriter keys striking down onto a piece of paper.
Typewriter. That's it! He rushed toward the body of the nearest Sapiens-Old and instantly melded with it, implanting his knowledge of the typewriter and how it worked. Pleased with his work, he waited around to see his Sapiens-Old begin to put his "invention" into being, building the first-ever typewriter on Amosulemat. Michael's job was done for the day, his inventions handed out, his fun completed…another Modien job was done, and in only five minutes. Paradise reigns after all.

Michael left the office building, stepping into an immaculate world. It was another beautiful day, just like every day. As he took his daily jaunt after work toward his car, and felt the sun beat down on his face and the wind blowing over his body and through his hair, he saw a small crowd gathering around a capuchin monkey on a unicycle next to a new attraction. "What is this big contraption that's creating quite a buzz?" he asked himself. "It looks like a roller coaster, but for hamsters." As he got closer, he started to understand the reason for all the hype. What had looked like hamster tubes were actually clear magnetic tubes, winding and twisting around each other with two openings, one an exit and the other an entrance. Michael could see people enter and then vanish, then after a few seconds they would exit with huge smiles on their faces. While the device looked intricate, he couldn't understand why all these people were lining up for it and coming out, stunned, then rushing back into line again.

"Hey, Michael," yelled out Gabriel, Michael's closest and best friend. "You have to check this out!"

"Hey, buddy, have the day off, I see. What is this thing?"

"Yup, I have the next couple days off, but this thing.... Words can't describe it, my friend. You'll just have to try it out for yourself."

"Ahhh, lucky, I can't remember the last day I took a day off. I'm quite intrigued as to what this thing could be—how could it make every one that goes through it so excited? Guess I'll just have to wait and see, though, right?" He stepped in line with Gabriel. "By the way, how's Angelina?" Michael asked as he flagged down an FFF. He put his hand into the sensor and, after the usual whirs, lights, and beeps, out popped a s'mores into Michael's hand. "Mmm just how I like them, soft and melted on the inside and crunchy on the outside."

Gabe laughed, "You and those S'mores. Angelina's doing great, thank you for asking. She's having a blast redesigning the house for Alexa and Elizabeth." Gabriel put his hand into the sensor of the FFF. More whirs, lights, and beeps, and a couple of slices of pizza popped out.

"Look who's talking," Michael laughed. "Can't argue with the classics, right?"

"Ha! Okay, you got me. You may have a point about the classics." Gabe chuckled as he started to eat his pizza. "Angelina couldn't be any happier with the twins coming."

"Ah, that's terrific. Tell her congrats and I hope to see the house once she finishes it. Better be worth the admission or I'm leaving." Gabriel laughed, knowing Michael was joking. "Hey, what's this like?" Michael continued as he gobbled down the rest of the s'mores. "There's dozens of tubes wrapping all around each other with nothing but empty space between them. I see everyone enter and exit, but nothing in between."

"It's like nothing I've ever experienced. This ride is going to change how we travel, even. It's something I'm sure the Old never had, or could dream of, for that matter. By the way, how is Jacob? I heard he got a … cold. How on earth did *he* get a *cold*??"

"I don't know," Michael answered as he and Gabe took another step or two forward in the line. "I didn't know the flu still existed, and how one could get to his house, even with all the security added since God left? The nanos would have detected the cold long before it even got there; I thought that's what they were designed for, to keep the Old from getting sick. I remember my dad telling me about the guy who invented the nanos and how it was such an amazing invention that no member of the Old ever got sick again. How the nanos patrol the world unseen, and can detect any harmful disease, virus, or anything that can infect the Old, and then destroy it."

"I thought the same thing until I heard about Jacob being sick. As far as I can remember, no other member of the Old has gotten sick before him. I haven't heard any other member of the Old sick, have you?"

"No. And of all the thousands of the Old still alive, what luck *he* would get sick. Which reminds me, I saw another guy that got dragged away from Satan today, yelling things like, "I must save it, I must save her, she needs me...." Could he have a cold, too?" Michael got lost in thought before suddenly seeing that it was Gabe's turn to go into this intriguing new machine. He shook his head and tapped Gabe's shoulder. "Anyway, it's your turn."

"I have no idea. I haven't heard much about *viruses* and *colds*, and anyway I got a new family to worry about now, no time to worry about such strange, ancient and rare things." He smiled and took a step with his back to the entrance of the machine and yelled out, "Buddy, you're in for quite a ride!" He turned around and jumped into the opening. Michael watched as Gabe's very body broke up into millions of pieces. His Vial of Viability got sucked up through the biggest of the tubes as the rest of his nano-bots rushed through the smaller tubes, disappearing out of sight. Michael heard some shouts of joy emanating from the tubes, fading to silence.

It was his turn now, but he hesitated for a second. Someone yelled out from the back of the line, "Hey man, just go for it!" Some of the crowd cheered, for they'd been through it already; the rest murmured with a growing anticipation. He took a deep breath and stepped into the doorway. His body, he felt, was getting lighter as a gust of wind whisked him through the tubes.

While inside, he felt the excitement and rush of a thousand roller coasters. He started seeing images of every wonderful thing that he had ever seen in his life flashing by his vision. Every memory and experience that made him feel alive coursed through him as his body was sucked through the tubes then sped along faster with the magnets. The tubes also coupled to intensify the whole experience tenfold by boosting every nano-bot's electrical signal instantaneously. His whole body, even though broken into millions of pieces inside the tubes, jolted with energy as he felt every good thing he has ever felt before all at once. It was such an intense and overwhelming feeling he now understood why everyone was running back in line again.

He saw his first dog, Dinky. How he laughed at as he used to poke the little indented white spot on top of her red head and call her "My little Dinky dog," and she would look back with that dog-smile of hers. He could feel all the years of happiness she brought to him. Next he saw his first love, Heather, and the time they spent together. He saw the day he met Marilyn and the look on her face when she said yes after he asked her to marry him. He also saw the day Amanda was born and all of his 340 years of life. All that love from them engulfed his feelings once again and flowed throughout his spirit, making him feel afire with a brand new life.

He experienced everything he had ever done in his A.T.M. Michael saw all those wonderful events and memories of his Sapiens-Old when they completed an invention that he gave them. They all seemed to flash by one at a time, yet it felt as though it took as long as it did to become a memory. It was incredible. "I could spend eternity in here," Michael thought.

A white light flashed over Michael's vision, and he saw the usual stretch of buildings on his way to and from work. He realized he was just outside the exit of the machine, and a huge smile broke upon his face. "Wow! That was amazing! How long was I in there?" He asked Gabe, who was waiting with a knowing grin on his face.

"Only a few seconds," Gabe replied.

"You're kidding me? It felt … it felt like years, though!"

"No, sir. The whole ride only takes three seconds to go through," said the inventor of the machine. "It uses the teleports we have to travel across the solar system, but they're in a fixed place. They are stretched throughout the inside of the magnetic tubes. I've got a license to have my own teleports for a year, but they only work within this structure. That was the deal I made with the High Committee of Invention Approval."

Astonished, Michael looked over at a smiling Gabe, then back at the man, and they both quickly ran to the back of the line for another turn. The man just smiled and watched them run off, then gestured to the next person that it was their turn.

"Incredible! I never felt anything like that before!" Michael exclaimed to Gabriel, after going through the new device again. "I wonder how he got the idea to invent it."

"I don't know, but I wish I would have thought of it."

"Me, too. Anyway, I was going to see my grandfather tomorrow and ask him what he remembers of colds and how dangerous he thinks his cold is."

"I've only seen colds while working with my Sapiens-Old," Gabriel mentioned. "But I never really paid attention to them. Have you?"

Michael pondered for a minute, as they continued walking to their cars. "No, not really. I was always focused on exchanging ideas and having fun. I never thought about the pains they experienced, because I never saw many. The people I did see that were sick would sneeze or cough as I walked by; that's all I remember. Even then I was told growing up not to interfere in the lives of the Sapiens-Old unless I was going to give one an idea. That made sense to me. Why would we want to dwell on the bad things they experience such as pain and sickness?"

"I agree. Who'd want to watch the Sapiens-Old suffer when they're sick, or worse, kill each other?" Just then Gabriel sensed his Modien Essence Transmitter sending a message from his wife. It appeared in his vision. "I gotta go, Michael. Angelina says come home quick because the twins are coming. Just let me know what Jacob remembers and wish for him to," he paused in his step and turned to Michael, "wish him to 'get well soon.'"

Michael smiled and thanked him. "Wow, they're coming already? Better get home, buddy. Hey, why'd you two decide to have twins, anyway?"

"Well, Angelina's grandmother was half of a set of twins, and *her* sister didn't make it through the Apocalypse. Angelina heard stories from her grandmother about how she and her sister would seem to know what the other was thinking, and could even share some of the feelings the other was experiencing. So, to honor to her grandmother, she asked if we could have twins, too. I couldn't resist that, not for my angel. I'm also quite curious myself to see how twins behave." He paused again and smiled. "I wonder if they will behave as the Sapiens-Old twins behaved? We even had the DNA made exactly the same for each. As far as I know, we're the first couple to have twins made with exactly the same DNA; all the other twins' DNA were slightly different."

"That's pretty cool, man. I want some pictures of them, and I'll be sure to tell my grandfather to 'get well soon.'"

Gabriel smiled. "You and those antiquated sayings like 'cool.' You're just like your father. He loved the days when the Old ruled the earth, all the different ways of life they had, and how he brought some of them for our society today to enjoy. Not only that, he created so many new things for us, like the Atomic Transference Machines. He truly was a man of vision and character." Another message set off in Gabe. "Ah, she doesn't want me to miss their birth, and wants to know what's taking me so long to get home." He entered his small, aerodynamic-looking vehicle which looked like a classic UFO-flying saucer. "Guess I'll have to design another car for all four of us now, too, huh? Or maybe I'll ask Angelina if she wants to do it since she loves designing new things."

Michael smiled, opening the door of his deep purple 1967 Pontiac GTO with dark green flames on the hood. He remembered his father and sighed. "Yeah, I guess so. Maybe I'll go and see Daniel too and ask if his father ever told him anything about colds or viruses."

"Good thinking." Just then Angelina sent Gabriel another message. "I gotta go!!" He waved to Michael, entered his car, and sped off.

Michael waved back, calling out congratulations as he watched Gabe disappear on the horizon in a flash. He entered his car, telling it to take him home. He rose off the ground next to a wall of metal that had an electromagnetic field around it. Michael stepped on the acceleration and the car revved up, sounding like the classic muscle car it was in the 1960's. It looked like an antique GTO, but its propulsion was outfitted with the latest technologically advanced engine, making it capable of flight at no cost to the environment, like every other mode of transportation in Modien society. He rose 400 feet and started soaring through a strong magnetic field, generated by the huge towers on the ground that were spread out over the landscape in every direction and were embedded into the structures of the buildings in the city.

Looking out the window, Michael saw the edge of the city off in the distance and birds flying along next to him as his ride soared through the air. Just then, his stereo started playing one of the songs he had acquired from the ancient times of the Old, Nickleback's *Rockstar*. He sat back to enjoy his ride home, remembering that incredible ride he'd gone through earlier. A big smile enveloped his face as he rode off to his home, relaxing after another hard day of work.

The Reuniting

At his apartment building, Michael stepped out of his car and watched it melt into the Recycler, to be rebuilt atom-by-atom again at his convenience, like everyone else's car. He entered the tube that lifted him up to his home; the sensors detected who he was and a gush of air blew him up through the tube, winding him through the building and straight to his door.

"Daddy!" Amanda ran up to Michael and jumped into his arms. "How was work today, Daddy? Tell me one of the ideas you gave to a Sapiens-Old."

He lowered her down, and walked over to their H.A.T.M.L., or Home Atomic Transference Machine, Limited. Its power was limited compared to the ones the Modiens used to create whole universes; therefore it could only create objects as big as a sofa or a car. He put his hand into the sensor and thought about a typewriter. Out popped a typewriter, and he handed it to her.

"What's this? It looks like a keyboard."

"Close," he started to answer as he walked over to the machine again, sticking his hand back in the sensor, a piece of paper falling out. He handed the piece of paper to her. "There you go. Let's see what you think this does." She quickly scanned the whole thing with a big smile on her face, then slipped the paper in the slot and started pressing down on the keys, typing something out. She proudly handed it to her father. "Pretty smart, Amanda. And you haven't even graduated school. You're going to do some amazing things with your A.T.M. That is, if you want to do what Daddy does." He read what she'd typed. "I think I can accommodate you with that," he said, giving her a big bear hug, lifting her up and spinning her around. She screamed with delight.

"Of course I want to have my own universe!" she exclaimed as she landed on her feet, pointing to the typewriter. "What's this thing called? They're fun! How come we don't have them? Was this from before the Switch?"

He chuckled. "Okay, okay. Well, first things first. It's called a typewriter, and yes, they were from the time before the Switch. And, I would say we don't use them now, because all we need to do is think of what we want to say, and the words are displayed in our vision or sent to someone. Very rarely do we use keyboards anymore; I only know of diplomats that use them still. We have robots now to build our structures and our thoughts tell our computers what to write and share. There was a time when people used their bodies more for things like typing on a typewriter to communicate with each other. It also took many strong and brave men to construct buildings back in the days of the Old, too; now our bodies are mostly for looks, it seems."

"Wow, is that all they had to use to communicate with each other, a typewriter?" she asked in astonishment.

Again Michael chuckled. "No, sweetie, they had many devices to talk with each other.... You'll find out more about how Modiens came to be, and how the Old used to live, next year. After you graduate, you're getting your own S.A.T.M. to have your very first Big Bang. Are you excited?"

"I can't wait! So I'll be able to start building my own universe with my very own Sapiens-Old?"

"You bet; you're just a year away. That's why it's extra important to learn as much as you can about how to get your structure for your universe to stay stable and how the rest of the universe works. Seems like it was only yesterday you were a little baby to me." He smiled and gave her another big bear hug and kissed her forehead. "You're growing up so fast; my dad told me it would be like this, but I had no understanding at the time. Anyway, where's your mother? I wanted to tell her Gabe is having twins."

"She went to Maui for a walk. She wanted to see the sunrise since she missed it rising here."

"She loves those sunrises. Will you be okay by yourself while I go and spend a little time with her?"

"DAD," Amanda replied declaratively, "I'm almost ten! I'll be fine! Besides, I have some homework to do anyway!"

"Oops, sorry darling," Michael said, forgetting again how much she'd grown up. "Well, we'll be back in about an hour, then. I'll look over your homework when I get back."

Michael left the house by jumping into the tube that rushed him up to the roof. He ran off the edge, jumping, yelling in enjoyment. He loved the feeling of the wind whisking throughout the sensors of his body, as do all Modiens. His nano-bots spread out ever so slightly, catching the wind and enabling him to gently land on the ground next to the travel center that was just down the block. "A perfect landing," Michael thought.

He told the robot behind the counter, which was behind a force field that protects each of the predestined teleports allowing Modiens to travel all over the solar system, that he wanted to go to Hawaii, the east cost of Maui, precisely. The robot scanned Michael's MET, confirming his identity and the clearance that allowed him to travel anywhere. A doorway appeared and the force field lowered. The robot wished him a safe and pleasant trip as Michael started stepping through the doorway. He stepped out just a few hundred feet from the beach.

He smelled the saltwater and heard the seagulls as he walked closer to the ocean. He sent a message to Marilyn asking where she was exactly because he was close. She replied that she was just down the street on the beach, and to hurry because the sun was just about to rise.

As he reached the shoreline, he saw her watching the waves crash against the sand, with the wind flowing through her long, dark-brown hair and the sun beating off her beautiful face. He walked up behind her and covered her eyes. "Guess who?"

She laughed and turned around, wrapping her arms around him, smiling, and gave him a gentle kiss. "Isn't this beautiful? I'm so happy you made it in time."

"I wouldn't have missed it for the world; you look beautiful today. How are you, sweetheart?"

"Better, now," Marilyn sighed in content as she rested her head on his chest. "Is Amanda okay alone?"

"Yes; she nearly had an overload when I asked her the same," he answered with a grin of amazement still. "I saw another man with a virus today. The third one I've seen since this month."

"Another! What's causing it?"

"I have no idea, but this guard said it was a virus like the other two I've seen. Tomorrow I'm going to see my father and grandfather and ask them what they remember of viruses and the flu. I can't think of those rare things, though, now. I don't even know why I brought it up. Right now I'm in heaven on earth." Michael wrapped his arms around her shoulder and kissed her forehead, and they both watched the sun slowly rise from the ocean.

"I have this feeling and I don't even know the words to describe it. As the Sapiens-Old might say, I'm, 'worried.'" She buried her head into his chest and sighed again. "I'm not as worried with you around, though."

"I hope you feel safe, baby; you mean the world to me, you and Amanda." Michael held her hand and waist a little tighter.

Marilyn exhaled in content. "Anyway, did you hear about Angelina having twins?"

"Yeah, Gabe told me today after I got off work; they're pretty excited about them, too. I didn't know Angelina's grandmother was a twin, did you?"

"Oh yeah, Angelina told me long time ago; she said not to mention it to anyone because her grandmother got upset and cried when I found out. I found out later from Angelina how upset her grandmother was; I don't know how she even knew we were talking about her sister, but she did. In fact, we shouldn't be talking about her now. She's a real nice woman. I met her and I don't want to upset her."

"Wow, that's amazing. I understand. I wouldn't want that to happen either. That makes me wonder if Gabe's twins will be able to sense that kind of thing, too. Speaking of something for the senses, I saw this amazing new invention today. I can't even describe it. Tomorrow I'll have to take you to it. It made me feel like a little kid again learning how the world works, my first Big Bang and the excitement of having my own universe, and then all my memories flushing over me.... I'm just stunned by it." He said, glowing with excitement, remembering.

"Wow, sounds incredible! What was it like?" Marilyn asked, looking up at him.

Michael smiled as he saw the sun sparkling in her hypnotic, dark-brown eyes. "I can't even describe it; it's so exhilarating and incredibly ingenious." He caressed her cheek and gave her a soft kiss. "Come on, let's go home. I can't wait for dinner I'm going to have some fried chicken, corn on the cob and mashed potatoes for lunch. I'll have something else for dinner that the FFF can make."

"Did you ... what's that word ... forget?"

Michael looked down at Marilyn, puzzled.

"I told you that I was going to arrange a special dinner for us tonight, remember?"

"Oh yes, of course. Wow, that's weird. I must have been going into a daydream of you." Michael brushed off the fact that he actually "forgot" something, something that Modiens never do, they never forget anything. He reassures himself that he was actually just about to daydream of Marilyn, that it was impossible for a Modien to forget anything, being a being of massive intellect and memory storage capability. He kissed her gently and reassured her that he was really okay.

"I hope so, sweetheart. Now let's go home; I want to see the look on Amanda's face when I tell her where we are eating for dinner."

"Sounds good; let's go." They walked back to the travel center holding hands. Michael thought to himself how perfect his life was and how lucky he was to have found Marilyn and have a smart and wonderful daughter like Amanda.

Michael and Marilyn got back to the house, but they didn't see Amanda. An hour went by and they really started to worry. They couldn't imagine why she wouldn't have her M.M.S. turned on, and they were about to go looking for her when Marilyn heard Brody bark. "Oh, there she is; she must have taken a walk." She saw Amanda walk in through the door. "Amanda, you didn't even leave us a note or tell us you were going. Why didn't you have your M.M.S. on?"

Relieved, Michael sat down, but once he did, another striking light bolted through his vision. He realized what this meant, and it wasn't good. He blacked out, once again with a worried look on his face, not knowing where he would be once he regained consciousness.

"Wake up, son!" Daniel shouted.

"What, where am I? I was just so relieved to see Amanda; she was missing."

"You're really tempting me, my boy, even though you're made from me, I will not hesitate to strike you down now and not even give you a chance to live and leave here. I've lost one son already; my soul is already empty. Losing you would just fuel my rage for losing Jeremiah and make me want to extract even more revenge from your beloved "God." Now, do you really want to know what your precious "God" said to me, Michael, or shall we get this over with?" Daniel smiled, raised his arm, pointed it at Michael and sparks flew off his fingertips.

Michael, still stunned from the recent jolt, but seeing that his father was very serious about killing him, said, "Yes, Father, I am sorry. I won't talk to you like that again." He closed his eyes, not wanting to see his death by the hand of his own father. Until that moment, Michael only thought of his own death by the way Modiens naturally die, by entering the Machine of Forever. Quite peaceful, no suffering or pain, and yet an image of countless people before him dying horrible, gruesome deaths sent chills throughout his body. He realized how lucky his kind was. His father didn't just want control and to show off that he could do what Satan couldn't, he wanted to inflict pain. "Please continue, I promise I won't use that tone again."

"Okay, then. Now, where was I before I got so rudely interrupted? Oh yes, there we were just sitting, eating dinner. There might have been some others around, I believe, I'm not quite sure, and I was having some delicious sushi, some masago rolls...."

"Oh, wow, that *is* some good stuff Dad; I so love the intricate details that are vital to the story ... 'Some others were around' you 'believe... not quite sure,' great details, and the sushi you were eating..."

Daniel sighed and sat down next to Michael, restraining himself. "He said to me, 'Daniel, I have a confession, I am not the being you think I am. I am not the God that you think I am.'"

"You're making this up! Why would He just blurt—"

"I wish I was making it up, son, I truly do. I even started to laugh because He does have a great sense of humor, actually. I thought He was setting up a big one, but then I looked into his eyes, and I knew it was no joke."

Michael looked over into his father's eyes and saw that he wasn't making this up. He realized the implications and thought, *What could his father possibly do with that information once he tells people of it*, then it hit him ... he wouldn't tell them right away. He was going to hold that back until God comes back once He has heard of Daniel escaping the Machine of Forever. He's going to use that against God to humiliate him. "So, then, what did He say?"

Daniel wrapped his arm around his son's shoulder. "He said that He's very sorry, and that He shouldn't have said that. He said He was told not to tell the people He helped make of the true story of what went on before humans, when the Old were around on Earth. He said in a somber tone that He was one of many that were allowed to create new beings on our planet. That He, along with several others, came to Earth long ago and sectioned off the planet to create Homo sapiens. They were given permission to teach them anything they could, to a certain degree of course, and help them evolve to a point until He and the rest of them had to leave and let their creations live on without them. They were to watch how they would get along with each other as some sort of experiment." Daniel picked up the glass of wine and took another sip.

"So, you're saying that God was one of many beings that created humans, and that they had rules to go by when teaching their creations the lessons of life, and that they had to leave when they were told. But by who?"

"He wouldn't say, or it didn't cross His mind to mention that part. You're doing well so far, but what you're saying is just repeating what I have said. Do you have anything original to add, any idea as to what happened to those early Homo sapiens and the beings that made them?

"Well, my guess is that those beings in that group that created Homo sapiens were *all* looked upon by their creations as "God?" That somewhere down the line all those beings became one, and that is God as we Modiens know Him to be?"

"Correct! Well, sort of. There were actually hundreds of religions and even more "Gods" throughout the existence of mankind."

"But that doesn't make sense; there's no record of any religions other than Christianity. And then God came back, just as it was foretold thousands of years before. That Jesus came back as God because Homo sapiens couldn't sustain the true nature of God's form. That Jesus is God; He's the one that came back to save us, just as—"

Daniel interrupted his perplexed child. "Don't you understand, son? It's all been covered up. Someone had to come back and challenge Satan when he tried to take over the very souls of the creations that they made. The way God told it, though, He made it seem like He was the only one left to try and come back and save all the creations. When He started to tell that part, a tear formed in his eye, and then He just stopped and left the room.

"Then how…"

"After the Apocalypse it was decided to keep the other religions suppressed from the new species. That "God" told everyone it was best for them not to know, and that He kept the records of all the religions that were around with orders that it be kept in secret until the appropriate time. I feel this would be the appropriate time to share that bit of information with the population, to see how they would deal with that."

"How is that possible, though? That makes no sense! There are too many members of the Old to keep quiet about all of that."

"That was the price they paid for the longevity of their lives, Michael," Daniel said with a heavy heart. "It was even made so that if one of the Old were to tell someone about the other religions, that person would die a horrible gruesome death before they could even finish their first sentence. Astonishing, isn't it? I found it hard to believe myself at first. I asked him how he could let something like that happen. He said it wasn't His choice that He had made a deal with Satan."

"God made a deal with Satan? But I thought God won the battle and Satan was imprisoned and his powers were taken away."

"They were, Michael. Here on New Earth. But you didn't think that he would be defeated so easily, did you? Awww, my poor boy, you did. You know, you should ask Marilyn if one of the requirements for being a diplomat is complete silence about what goes on with the other civilizations they go to when they're assigned to them. You poor thing, you probably don't even know that some of the diplomats aren't even the original people that you know of, they're clones of themselves. I wonder if Marilyn even knows that, or maybe she'll just find out the hard way."

A blinding orange light flashed over Michael's vision. His first reaction was to try to attack his father for saying such things. It was a reaction he'd never felt before, this anger. But it was quickly squelched with an overwhelming calm feeling. "No, I didn't know that. Why do you think God told you all those things if He wasn't allowed to?"

"He said He felt guilty and wanted us to know. He wanted to tell the truth because He felt it was the right thing to do. Too bad, though; sometimes telling the truth doesn't always mean something good will come from it. I've had more than enough time to think about this, and *I feel* that telling you is the right thing to do. And I will tell others that I trust and together we will bring back a long lost art, long forgotten by our kind."

"Who are these people, Father?"

Daniel burst out laughing, got up from the chair and slapped Michael on his back, causing another shock of electricity to course through their bodies. Michael shouted in pain as Daniel cringed and gloated with a slight look of pleasure on his face at inflicting that pain. "Do you really think I'm going to divulge that kind of information to you? You're still a funny child, Michael. I can't help but laugh at some of the things you say some times."

"So that's it? God was part of a group of beings given permission to create humans? Is that why you think there's no God?"

"Oh, I never said there *was no God;* just that the one you think is God, isn't. He is a fraud, a liar, the ultimate deceiver of man. He lied to all of you, and worst of all, He lied to *me!*"

Michael burst out laughing now. "You really are arrogant, Father, always making everything about you."

"Don't you understand, son? I was supposed to be the perfect being. I was the first Modien, and I was the one He trusted most out of everybody, including the Old! But as He failed me in the premature killing of my wife and son, I shall make him fail. He thought He created the perfect being; He was only half right!

"What are you talking about Father? We are perfect."

"So perfect that He chose for us to die after 800 years? No, He doesn't care about us. It always has to be about Him! He's the only one that can live forever. You think it was a coincidence that He was the one that came back to save us? You think that throughout human history there weren't other wars before the Apocalypse? And I'm not just talking about the battles between Homo sapiens, I'm talking about all those "Gods" throughout time that were also battling with each other. They wanted control over the human soul they helped create. What you also don't know is that there have been many other excavations from times of the Old that show of such battles between those "Gods," but have you heard of such things of the past? No, you haven't. The Homo sapiens at the time would see those battles and record them. Battles occurring all throughout time, and yet that information was concealed."

"Who gave the authority to not make that information public?"

"Who do you think, Michael? He said such information would cause panic amongst the people. Imagine what the people will think of their precious God when they hear that not only was He not *"God,"* but one of *many* beings that created the Old, and in essence, ourselves. Imagine the chaos that will bring, especially when the rest of the Modiens hear that they were lied to by someone essentially like themselves. Someone they believed was God. Their Creator. Do you think they will stand for such atrocities?"

"No," Michael said reluctantly. "I am still in shock and don't know how to react myself. But I don't feel angry, and I don't know if anyone else will, either. So, in my opinion, Father, I feel this is all in vain."

"Oh Michael, you're probably right; no one will get angry from this information. I know that those kinds of emotions have been genetically altered to stop occurring as much as possible, if at all, and that people will see Him as more of a God than ever, giving sympathy toward Him for being so honest and courageous. That's just who we are ... excuse me, *you* are. Sometimes I forget that I've passed on."

"So why go through with this, then, Father? Why not just live with that information and the mindset you had when you first heard the truth from Him? What's changed in you, Dad? What is it inside you that you have to extract this revenge for losing Jessica?"

"Jessica?" Daniel responded with curiosity and astonishment. "Jessica, Michael? Really? *She IS your mother!* How *dare you* call her by her first name! Just because you never knew her doesn't mean you aren't a part of her! Don't *ever* forget that, *Michael*."

Michael thought, "That was wrong of me, but I can't admit to that, it will only boost his already inflated ego. Besides, what more could he possibly do to me; if he really wanted to kill me, he would have by now."

Daniel stood up once again and walked over to a window. "Why do you hate me, Michael?"

"Hate you? I never even thought that I could hate you. Why would you say...?"

Before Michael could finish, Daniel said, "You don't have to say it, Michael, I can feel it. There is a lot of hate building up in you now. There is a lot of resentment and fear. It's okay to have those feelings, my boy. Trust me, I know all too well about them."

"You don't know anything, Father. Most certainly you don't know my own feelings. I have to laugh at your assumption there, Father."

"That's laughter of defense. You hate the fact that I'm telling you all this. You hate the fact that it is probably true and you hate that you and everyone you know were lied to by someone you loved and trusted. I can feel the hatred boiling inside you. I can see it in your eyes."

"You know nothing!" Michael shouted, causing him to move too much, and again he was jolted by the electric chair, only to wake up in the real world.

"I know, and I'm sorry, Mom," Michael heard Amanda apologize and realized he was once again back in real life, no longer suffering from these powerful and realistic daydreams. "I know I should have let you know, but Brody got out somehow when I was working on my speech and listening to my music. It all happened so fast." She unhooked a frantic Brody off the leash and the big black beauceron rumbles over to Michael who pets him and calms the big loveable dog down. "One second I'm cruising along writing my speech, the next thing I look up and see him somehow open the door and run out. I ran after him but just missed grabbing him before he went down the air tube! I was going to jump in after him but the tube I went in took me to the roof. It took a while to find him again after I landed, but when I did I took him for a walk. I'm sorry. I should have at least turned on my M.M.S. It won't happen again, I promise."

Marilyn walked over to Amanda and hugged her. "Okay, darling. I'm just glad you're all right. We were really worried. Anyway, I want to hear all about your speech and what have you been up to. I've missed you dearly. It seems like forever since I was home."

"Awww Mom, it's only been a couple weeks, but I missed you, too. I don't know if anything is new, although I did just come up with this great quote for my speech."

"That's wonderful, baby, I'm so proud of you. What's the quote?"

Amanda scoffed, "Oh Mommy, nice try. I'm not letting this gem out to anyone before my speech. Sorry."

Marilyn giggled, "Okay angel, fair enough. Hey, are you hungry?"

Amanda let go of her mother's waist and looked up with a smile on her face. "Always, Mommy, but I can get it. What do you want?" She called over the FFF.

"No, sweetheart. Don't bother, and get your coat. Let's go out to eat."

"Wow, really?" Amanda could already guess the places that her mother had in mind "Is it the Maze of Inter-dimensional Aliment or the Tower of Food? Those two are my favorite of anywhere to eat at! Oh boy!"

"Well, tonight I thought we'd go to the Tower of Food. Is that all right?"

"Wooooooo hoooooo, you bet it is! I can't wait!"

They headed over to the Tower of Food, located on the outskirts of Aeon. When they arrived, they told the machine what they wanted. Michael chose Indian food; some vegetable samosa's, saag paneer, and lamb biryani. Marilyn picked some Italian; A Caesar salad, gnocchi, and finally some tiramisu. Amanda picked a random meal. The bot told them to have a good meal, and then they soared off on a platform miles into the sky. Once at the top, they looked at the incredible view, seeing for hundreds of miles in any direction. "Well, who's first?" asked Marilyn.

"ME!" shouted Amanda. She hugged them both and jumped off the platform, plummeting down miles to the bottom. "Here comes the first ring...yum Caesar salad...." She saw little lettuce plants sprouting out of thin air below, then fall apart into a lake of dressing. As she continued to fall, she saw croutons rain down like hail and she passed through, munching on it all. "Wow! They have the best Caesar salad ever! Mmmmm, it's got such crisp lettuce and delicious tasting dressing!

"The next ring is coming up quick, French onion soup …" It instantly appeared a fraction of a second before Amanda passed through the ring. Her body absorbed the soup instantaneously wherever it came in contact with it. "Mmmmm the melted cheese is so good with the bread and the savory onion taste makes my senses come alive!"

"Here comes the main course!" She saw chicken nuggets popping up around her as she fell through the third ring. She started to fly through the nuggets, munching on each one by plucking them out of the air and dipping each one in a variety of sauces. These she actually popped into her mouth. "Mmmmm, the marinara sauce is real tangy, such a great counterbalance to the sweet and sour sauce. Ooooo, I can't wait for dessert."

Finally, as she sailed down to earth, she saw the last ring. "Yay! It's banana split time!" Amanda could hardly contain herself. She saw a fountain of chocolate syrup with sprinkles and nuts flowing through it, then the bananas shot across her path, and some cherries on top of whipped cream clouds formed beneath her. She fell through each scrumptious layer, enjoying every flavor of the flying banana split.

Marilyn and Michael followed behind quickly, enjoying their own meals as they passed through the rings. "Wow, that was some on the best Indian food I've ever had," declared Michael. "How was your meal, ladies?"

"Terrific, Daddy! I got a banana split this time for my dessert. I was hoping for tiramisu, but you can never go wrong with a banana split. How was your dinner, Mommy?"

"Perfect, as always—never had better clams casino. I'm stuffed. Let's go home now. I have to prepare some Titan documents for Crystal in case I get the diplomat's job. Is that okay with everyone else?"

"Of course, hon; I was going to help Amanda with her homework, anyway. She's been having trouble sustaining the structure of her universe."

"Oh, Daddy. I was hoping you wouldn't say that. I was hoping to have it done by the time Mom got home."

Marilyn picked up Amanda and gave her an Eskimo kiss. "You don't worry about impressing me! I just want you to get it right in the end. That's what is the most important to me. I know you're going to solve that problem soon enough; then you'll breeze through the rest of school with ease, I just know you will."

Amanda developed a smile from ear to ear. "Awww, Mom. I love you. I'm going to do my best to do the right thing and solve the problems that come my way, no matter what they may be. I bet I can even one day be a diplomat, like you. That is, after I have my own universe, like Daddy."

Marilyn put Amanda down between her and Michael, and took both their hands, leading them back to the teleport and home.

That night, Michael saw an image pierce his mind like nothing before as he walked into the family room. He saw Amanda inside the electrified cage where Satan was held. He saw the Pother gone and the form of a man was whispering in Amanda's ear and pointing back to Michael over her shoulder. He saw Amanda make a face like he had never seen on a Modien before, but that he had seen when Sapiens-Old got mad at each other.

Satan then took Amanda's hand, and together they walked out of the cage. He smiled at Michael as they disappeared into the crowd of people, who still only saw the Pother, since they were told not to look too long. Michael screamed, "No, I must save it! I must save her! She needs me, she needs me!" He started running through the people trying to chase down Amanda and bring her back home. He pushed people aside in a frantic search for his one and only child, but to no avail. He shoved one man aside who was blocking his view just after he thought he saw them, and then, suddenly, he was in his living room again. Marilyn and Amanda were sitting at the table; Amanda doing her homework and Marilyn waiting to correct it.

Marilyn stopped working on her own project for Crystal, looking up at Michael. "What's wrong? What is it, baby?"

"I ... I don't know; I don't remember," Michael replied, still dazed and confused. "I saw Amanda, but she didn't seem like herself. Then she just disappeared and I couldn't find her."

"Awww, sweetie." Marilyn brought him into her arms and ran her fingers through his black, curly hair. "She's right here in the family room with me. I'm helping her with her homework. She hasn't gone anywhere."

"I know, but it felt so real. I felt like I was having a daydream, and I was just standing here watching you two then I just saw her disappear right in front of me. I couldn't do anything about it in time."

"You yelled out, 'No I must save it, I must save her, she needs me.' What was that about?"

"I said that?" Michael paused as he remembered that was what, earlier that day, the man had said as he was being dragged away from the Cage of Satan. "I don't remember that." He decided not to mention the fact that he said the same thing the man with the virus had said as he was being arrested and dragged away to an unknown destination. "Well…. I'm fine, it's probably nothing."

"Are you sure? You seem nervous."

"Yeah, I'm fine, don't give it another thought. What are you studying tonight, Amanda? I know I was going to help you tonight, but Mommy said she'd help because she missed you so much. Are you sure I can't do anything to help?"

"Yes, Daddy. I'm sure. I didn't go anywhere, silly. I've been here the whole time. Are you sure you're okay, Daddy?"

"Yes, angel, I'm fine. I promise. Please, don't stop doing your homework."

Marilyn and Amanda looked at each other and both smiled in relief. "I'm trying to learn how to create the structure my universe will start in, but it keeps falling apart in my simulations. I can't figure out what I'm doing wrong."

Smiling as he remembered that he had had that same problem as a nine-year-old, he said, "You will get it. I can see you're so close to finding the solution; you're doing great. Sometimes to solve something you're having difficulty with, you have to take a step back from what you're working on, or even just stop trying to solve it altogether, and out of the blue the solution comes to you. Sounds silly, huh? Trust me, it works. Never give up, though."

"But isn't stopping altogether giving up? It sounds the same to me."

"Well, you're right," he smirked. "I misspoke … I meant that sometimes you could be trying too hard, and that sometimes taking a break from the problem and doing something that's relaxing and completely different can help a lot."

"I'll start right now!" She called out for Brody. "Can we go to the park to play for a while?"

"Of course you can, sweetheart. Just, please, keep your M.M.S. on this time," replied Marilyn as she stood up to give her a hug.

"Will do! Thanks, Mom. Bye, Dad. Come on, Brody!" Amanda ran out of the house and off to the park. Marilyn turned to Michael and gave him a kiss.

"Now, are you sure you're okay?" Marilyn asked her husband. "I hope you didn't get that virus that poor man had."

Michael laughed, figuring even if a virus was contagious he had been too far from the guy to get it. There were people a lot closer than he had been to the man; if anyone would have a virus, it would be them. He thought to himself how the guards would probably get the virus first if it was contagious, and he had seen them since that incident. They seemed perfectly fine. "I'm fine; I'm just thinking about my grandfather and how he has caught a cold. So strange to even hear of an actual cold … I've only heard about them in school … and how while inside the A.T.M., we're not to be around any Sapiens-Old that have had a cold for too long. I never knew why, though. I'm going to see him tomorrow and maybe my father, too. It's so strange that his nanos didn't detect his cold and get rid of it before he even got sick. They've been working since early in the First Generation; no member of the Old has gotten sick since they were invented."

Marilyn shuddered uncontrollably with a chill, not knowing the cause. "Well, tell Jacob I miss him and can't wait to hear one of the stories of when he was younger again, and I hope this cold of his isn't too serious.'"

"I will. Are you cold?" Michael asks, feeling her shake in his arms. "Want me to turn the air up?"

"No, I'm fine. I don't know what that was. But now that Amanda's gone, let's have some fun." She looks deep into his eyes and kisses him.

The next day, Michael got in his car and heard the notes of one of his favorite antiquarian songs that's survived over a thousand years, Sublime's *Santeria*. He programmed his grandfathers' house into the car and sat back, relaxing, singing along as the car drove itself to its destination, soaring hundreds of feet above the ground. Looking at the massive buildings passing by, all the people and the attractions, he suddenly fell into another trance.

People were running and screaming, some catching on fire and slowly dissolving away into nothing. He shook his head and yelled out, "Stop! Stop! No more!" And as quickly as the images had come into his mind, they left. Just then the car stopped, and his door opened in front of his grandfather's house. He didn't even remember passing the guard or passing through the two portals of the force field protecting he Old from the outside world. "Wow, what's going on with me? This is a different vision—no white light and my father afterward. I wonder why I'm getting two different types of visions. At least I'm safe now, and at my grandfathers' house."

Inside the Forest of the Old

Jacob had a beautiful place with a lush garden filled with all sorts of exotic plants surrounding it, and a pool in the backyard. This was only a small part of the 100-acre property he lived on. He kept many different types of species as pets, ranging from dogs and fish to some animals that had been recreated from the days of his youth but actually never survived the Impact. Jacob, as did others, spawned them from blood samples that had been kept in storage. His place was one of thousands given to the Old. The land grants comprised a vast area, almost a third of the country which was once known as America.

Michael saw his grandfather sitting on his favorite chair, feeding the ducks in the little pond in front yard. Michael dodged a duck that had broken away from the flush and headed off over the trees. He thought to himself how odd it was that only one duck flew off while the rest were too interested in being fed. "Who knows how animals think and what their plans are?" Michael amused himself with that thought, and then shook his head in hopes of forestalling any horrible visions. He focused on enjoying where he was, out in the country.

"Michael, it's been so long. How are you?" Jacob stood up and stretched out his arms to give his grandson a hug. "Are you okay? You look panicky." He started to cough uncontrollably and quickly headed back to his chair to rest.

Michael helped him sit down. "I'm fine, Grandpa. Don't worry about me. How are you, though? Is that coughing from your cold?"

"I'm afraid so." He coughed a little bit more, bringing his handkerchief to his mouth and spitting up some phlegm. He sighed and leaned back in his chair. "I haven't had a cold in … I can't remember how long, must have been just after the Switch. Wow," he laughed, "a thousand years already. I would never have thought I'd live so long; it's so overwhelming sometimes." He looked over at Michael and touched his face. "Amazing! You feel just like me, but you're nothing like me, really. Hard to imagine something so beautiful as your species could exist. You have such wonderful lives in such an incredible world." He coughed again. "I'm dying, Michael … I can feel it coming soon. But would I really die? You are told your M.E.T. will be absorbed into the Ball of Essence and you'll experience heaven and all that, just like my son did when he passed on...." Jacob paused, thinking to himself how a parent should never outlive child, and then he continued in a somber tone. "And that people like me, the Old, will also be a part of the Ball of Essence. But what is recording my life now? What part of me is going to be absorbed into the Ball of Essence so that I can experience my heaven? God said that it's all just energy and we, the Old, shouldn't worry about such things, that there is a reason for everything. I'm told I won't really know or care that I'm just a program, though, and that I'll feel as though life is infinite and anything I could imagine and create will be available to me at any time I want. But in the end, I'll just be a memory. In all my years, I wondered what death would be like. It's hard to imagine such things, no?" Before Michael could answer, Jacob continued, "Do you know what I'm going to miss the most, Michael?"

"No," Michael replied with a puzzled look. He'd never actually experienced someone sick and dying.

"I'm going to miss learning new things," Jacob replied. "Ah, after all these years I think that learning new things is the key to life, adaptation. Adaptation is something I've learned you people have sort of phased out. You people can control the weather, and make any type of food taste how you want with your Flying Food Fabricators. You can even make any animal imaginable just by thinking about it and having machines reconstruct its DNA. You can create whole universes for people *like me* to live in! Oh, sure, once in a while someone you love has to go away, turned into a memory like I'm going to be. Or a new invention changes how you grow your food or creates an experience of something fun, new, and exciting.... You might have to adapt to that, but it's not the same as it was in my day. There was more chance in life, I guess. BAH, don't listen to an old man like me! You probably have no idea what I'm talking about anyway. It's not your fault, my boy, it's just the way things are now. How is your family? How old is Amanda now ... seven?"

Michael was taken aback by what he'd just heard. He'd never really thought of how different his grandfather's life had been before he Switch, compared to his own. He wondered what his grandfather's concept of adaptation was, not really understanding the whole thing at all. He was so lost in thought that he couldn't remember Amanda's age for a minute. "No, she's nine now, about to graduate and get her own starter A.T.M. and have her very first Big Bang."

Jacob started laughing, causing him to cough again. "Atomic Transference Machines ... amazing feats of engineering, never thought I'd see those, either, but then again I never thought any of this would happen to me."

"Any of what?" asked Michael.

"Just all of it, God and Satan being real, the Apocalypse, Atomic Transference Machine, living to be over a thousand, you name it. I would never have imagined any of it in all my years of life. I feel very lucky indeed. Your kind gets to live to be 800. Mine was lucky to even be born at all, let alone to live to be my age now, or even a fraction of it." Jacob stopped talking and tossed some more bread at the ducks, who quacked for more.

They sat quietly and reflected on life for a few minutes, watching the ducks eat the rest of food and preen themselves.

The reality of Jacob passing sank in. He put his head down on his hand and sighed.

"Hey, now, none of that. You can still see me, right? I'll be around whenever you want to come visit me, like now. I just won't be able to come see you. I'm sorry I haven't made it out there in a while, I just feel so run down lately. But, whatever, it's all gravy, I'm still kicking."

Michael burst out laughing. "Gravy? How does everything being gravy relate to you dying … or anything, for that matter?"

Jacob started laughing, too. "I forget you Modiens have it made already. Every day has been gravy since the Switch."

"I guess … but what does that mean?" Michael asked, still laughing some.

"Life was tough back when my kind ruled. The majority of the population actually starved; most of the rest worked hard to get food like meat and potatoes…."

Before Jacob could say any more, Michael asked, "But what's the saying mean, Grandpa? We all have meat and potatoes AND gravy. I don't understand the big deal—you had them all, too."

"Heh, you have always been impatient, always wanting to hear the ending before the whole story is told. Even as a kid you would ask 'How's it end?' Well, Mr. Impatient, gravy, as you know, is added to food to make it taste even better. It's a luxury, really. Nowadays you Modiens have food anytime and anywhere you want. What, with those Flying Food Fabricators you have, food comes as easy as flagging one down. Now, when I lived, food wasn't as available. Most Homo sapiens starved. Now, Modiens, well…." He stopped and looked over at Michael, who just wasn't getting it. He smiled. "Well, I'm just happy you are here and that I'm still around to see my own grandson right now. Could you bring Marilyn and Amanda by one day soon? I'd like to see them before I pass on. I'd still like to have some more memories of them to relive when I'm gone.

I don't quite get how everything I've gone through can be recreated inside the Machine of Forever. It amazes me how anything I can imagine or want to recreate can be acquired simply by thinking of it, and the Machine of Forever will make it. Who knows what really happens until it happens, right? All this talk about food, though, has made me hungry. How about some pizza?"

Michael smiled. "You got it. Where's your FFF?"

"Bah! That thing is on the fritz again."

"Why don't you just put it in your H.A.T.M.L. and have it fixed?"

"I'll never learn how to fix anything myself if I just throw whatever's broken into that contraption and out pops a brand new one."

Michael sees the logic in his grandpa's case and thinks he should start doing the same. "Where's your FFF now, though? You know, since we're hungry, we can fix it with the H.A.T.M.L. just this one time, okay?"

"You're so precious, Michael; don't ever change. Last I saw, it was in the living room. What toppings do you want?"

"Sausage, pepperoni, and green peppers, please," replied Michael, as he headed inside to the living room. "What about you?"

"That sounds great to me, I'll be here waiting."

He found his grandfather's Flying Food Fabricator and put it inside the H.A.T.M.L. There were the usual whirs and beeps, and within seconds a brand new, working FFF floated out. Michael put his hand in the sensor of the FFF, and out popped a fresh, steaming pizza. He brought it out to Jacob on the patio and they sat quietly, eating. Michael, of course, finished before Jacob, being able to just touch a slice to eat it, not caring how hot it was.

"I'm still amazed how you eat … looks fun. Can you really taste with any part of your body?"

"Grandpa …" Michael answered, laughing. "We've talked about this before—of course I can, and it *is* really fun."

"Ah, that's right. Forgive me, Daniel. I'm old. I forget things sometimes."

Michael sat there, debating whether to correct him. He decided to let it pass. "Hey, Grandpa, I saw another man with a virus this week. Only this man was dragged away for going INSIDE Satan's Cage! The other two people I saw that had a virus were victims of looking at the Pother for too long, the guards said that the Halo of Ataraxia had stopped them before they could get inside the Cage of Satan, and that it also stopped them from being fully influenced by Satan and that they were fine now. Why would that one man want to go get so close to such a being trapped inside an electrified field? Didn't he know he could have died from the field overloading his circuitry?"

"I have no idea why on Earth—excuse me—New Earth, anyone would want to get so close to that thing! Even as weak as it is now, I still remember what he was capable of doing. The man must be sick indeed. Crazy, even!"

"What? What is this? Modiens can go crazy, too?" Michaels' only experiences with "crazy" were with the rare Sapiens-Old that he'd seen talking to themselves in one of his universe's cities. He wondered if *they* saw images like he had, and if he was going crazy.

Jacob started laughing. "How should I know? You're the Modien, here. I haven't heard of any one going crazy, not since he Switch at least, let alone a Modien. I didn't know myself that your species *could* go crazy. You all seem so … perfect." He started coughing uncontrollably again and asked Michael to leave because he needed his sleep. He reminded him to come back soon with the entire family. Michael agreed and helped him to bed, telling him that Marilyn and Gabriel wished him to get well soon.

Jacob smiled. "I haven't heard that in ages. I love you, son. Give Marilyn and Amanda my love. I look forward to seeing them soon."

"Okay, Grandpa. Get some rest. I love you, too." Michael kissed his forehead and left the room, pulling the door closed on his way out. He stepped outside the house and thought about what he'd heard, wondering if he *was* crazy. He didn't want to see his father and deal with getting ignored by him again, especially not after hearing that his grandfather is going to die soon. With nothing else to go by, he figured he wasn't crazy and not wanting to go crazy visiting his father, he headed off to work, even though he'd be quite early.

Sitting in the break room of the office, Michael went over what he'd experienced in the past couple of days. His head in his hands, he looked down at the table, wondering what the man could have seen or heard to make him want to go into that cage … what was so important that he was willing to risk his life being in such a strong electrical field like that? Who was "she" that he must save? And what did it have to do with the visions he was having?

Just then, Gabriel walked in. "Wow, you're here early, and you look different. Are you okay?"

"Oh, I'm fine. I just have a lot of things on my mind lately, is all. I'm depressed about Jacob dying and wondering how these people can have viruses, and just…." He paused. He thought maybe it wasn't the best idea to share the vision of Amanda talking with Satan and then walking outside the cage with him into the world.

"Just what? Wait, what? Jacob is dying? I thought it was just a cold!"

"I thought so, too, but when I went to go see him, he told me he was dying, that he can feel it coming."

"Oh, wow. That's terrible news. I'm so sorry to hear that. It feels like he's my grandfather, too; I've known him as long as I've known you. What's it now, 334 years? I, I don't know what to say. Hopefully he'll be okay and get over this cold he has. I mean, he's a tough man that's been through a lot, right?" Gabriel asked uncertainly.

"Yeah, 334 years. Wow, it's been that long? Incredible. I hope Jacob will be okay, too, and he *is* a tough old man, I have to say that. I mean, whoever survived the Apocalypse must be strong. Being a part of him and what he stands for, gives me strength."

Gabriel stopped to think about what it must have been like for the Old, and how terrible it must have been seeing everyone they loved die in front of them, the horrors they must have experienced before God came back to save the human race. He wondered how Satan was able to influence an entire species into thinking that evil was actually good. He was thankful that Satan couldn't seduce his kind, and couldn't influence the Old anymore, either. He was thankful that after Satan was vanquished, his powers became contained inside the electric field. He was also curious about how Angelina's grandmother survived the Apocalypse but her sister didn't.

Gabriel stopped thinking completely, which is quite hard to do for a Modien, for he saw a vision of his beloved Angelina and the new twins. The three were in a stone room with very little light breaking through animal skin curtains. Angelina was holding one of the twins trying to calm it down and Gabriel saw a man who raised a wand above her head, bringing it down over her head. He heard a cry like no Modien had ever made. A sound that he thought came out of one twin's mouth, but the power and force behind it was something an infant couldn't produce on its own. It was a groan so loud it shook the earth itself; some stones fell, letting more light in, and Gabriel saw a look of pure horror on one of his daughter's faces, while the other's shone with a bright, giggling smile.

The looks on both their faces confused and horrified Gabriel. Angelina that was struck by the Halo of Ataraxia fell behind the chairs of the twins and out of sight from Gabriel. He shook his head and, just for a split second, he saw Michael inside the break room looking at the desk in deep thought as if he, too, were experiencing a daydream.

An instant later, another scene raced across his vision. He saw the man of blonde hair who looked very familiar, but Gabe couldn't think of where he could have seen him before, which was odd for a Modien, because they always remember everything and everyone they meet. He saw the man walking up to Daniel holding the wand that produces the Halo of Ataraxia and a burlap sack, handing Daniel the sack and shaking his hand.

Daniel opened the sack, looked inside, smiled and looked up at Gabriel. He handed the sack back to the stranger after he cinched it up, and started to walk casually over toward Gabriel, still smiling. "I thought you might show up, which is why I took the precaution of taking your brand new twins. Now, I know what you're thinking, and it … could … be true. Which is why you must not think about trying to interfere with me, my son. Otherwise, well, you already know what I'll do to them, don't you."

Gabriel stopped in his tracks, thinking about the lives of his daughters and wife, and agreed to walk away from this situation. He rationalized to himself that if Daniel wanted to hurt them, he would have by now; he just had to bide his time to try to save them at a later date. "Daniel, please…."

Before Gabriel could utter another word, Daniel said, "Shhh, don't press your luck any further, son." Daniel motioned for the stranger to stop walking and to hold the sack up. "You are very level-headed, Gabe. You can always see both sides of the situation before jumping to conclusions, which is why I think you've excelled. Now, before you rush to judgment here, think it through. Don't react to something that will regret from now until the end of time."

Suddenly a white light flashed before his vision. Not being able to feel his legs, Gabe suddenly jolted up from his chair and sent it flying back to the wall.

He was back in the break room, and his family was not in sight. Gabriel saw Michael sitting there in deep thought, not even realizing what happened just next to him. He started to feel scared and cold. It was something he'd never felt before.

He asked for the feelings to be taken away. A warm rush of energy flowed throughout his body, making him feel calm and safe again.

Quickly the memory of that vision disappeared from Gabriel's mind, and he wondered what happened to his chair and why he was standing. He got the feeling that he had seen Michael sitting there just like that before, and seeing the chair knocked over on its side against the wall, but he didn't remember why, since he couldn't remember how his chair got that way or why he was standing up. He decided it was nothing and asked, "Now, what's this other business of yours that's leaving you all knotted up? I can sense it's something important...." He tapped Michael on the shoulder, seemingly waking him from a dream, and he turned to look back up at Gabriel. "And since you told me about Jacob possibly dying and passing on, it must be something pretty big."

Still unwilling to share the visions *he* has had with his best friend, Michael replied, "Just life," he answered in a defeated tone. "I'm just wondering about death, is all. It's one of the rare times in my Modified-Sapiens life that I'll have to adapt to something, or so Jacob tells me. He says our ability to manipulate pretty much anything we want, like growing any type of food or animal, or even controlling the weather, has left us without the skill to adapt. That adaptation is slowly being phased out of our human nature. I'm also wondering how these people are getting viruses. Are they just looking at the Pother for too long, or are they developing the viruses beforehand? I just don't know anything anymore."

Gabriel picked up the chair and sat next to his best friend. He slapped his back. "Hey now, I don't know what's going on either, but I know what will make us feel better: let's go to work. I'm giving someone on one of my worlds the idea of an airplane today," Gabe said anxiously.

"That's pretty cool, man. I guess I should do something new today, too. Maybe it will make me feel better." They got up and headed off to their respective A.T.M.s. "See ya in 5," Michael told his friend as they both entered their doorways. As soon as he saw the keyboard to his A.T.M. in front of him, Michael smiled with the familiarity of it, and the anticipation of seeing his creations once again set in. Gabe was right. Michael felt good as new.

A small point of light appeared in front of Michael as a feeling of weightlessness overwhelmed him. The little point of light grew bigger and bigger. He saw his Big Bang explode again, and then his universe expanded around him and inflated off to an unimaginable distance.

Once again, after his universe started up, the A.T.M. loaded up the date to the split second where Michael last gave an idea for each of his civilizations and input the last planet he was on. Nothing new had changed for his creations, though. They felt no pause in time at all and had no idea their lives could even be put on hold while their creator was off the clock. As far as the residents were concerned, it was business as usual. Michael admired the view of the scale and beauty of his universe.... "Remarkable," he said. "It looks exactly like the universe I live in, only it's filled with *my* Sapiens-Old. Hmmm, since Gabe's going to give the airplane as an idea to one of his Sapiens-Old, I think I'm going to do something that's never been done in my universe before, too, but what?"

After thinking for a second or two, Michael decided he would have one of his people invent space travel. "I wonder how these people will interact with the first civilization they find and what those people will think of these beings coming down from the sky. I can't wait!"

After looking over which of his planets was the most technologically advanced, he found the one and descended through its atmosphere. He landed just on the outskirts of an urban city, stepped out of his protective A.T.M. room, took a deep breath and cringed at the smell. He kept forgetting how badly the pollution can be sometimes on some of his planets, and reminded himself to also give these people clean-energy technologies.

The Sapiens-Old, it seemed, was a stubborn breed, Michael had noticed, not very open to change, even if it was for the better of their species. Their DNA had the "evil genes," those that produced greed and envy, still activated, so the dark forces of Satan could easily influence them.

Michael sat down on a park bench in the middle of one of the biggest cities on the planet and just watched his people, studying them this time instead of just experiencing the good things in their lives or giving them ideas. He started noticing how they behaved toward each other, and how they barely talked as they passed by one another. Those that did talk sometimes yelled and threatened others. It was not often he saw people laughing or smiling. He couldn't understand these behaviors. He couldn't grasp how the same species could treat each other so badly. "Even animals don't treat their own kind in such abusive ways," he thought.

He saw a man not unlike himself, only a bit younger. A young boy that looked slightly younger than Amanda ran up to the man. The two started talking. They seemed to be father and son. After looking more closely at them, he saw how they both looked dirty, really dirty, and pale. He realized they were homeless. This was the first time he'd actually seen a homeless person and he was not sure how to feel.

"Look at these people—the vast majority of them just walk by, not helping this man and his son. I have to do something." He decided to make this man the recipient of the knowledge to invent the first space-traveling vehicle for this planet. Instead of melding with this Sapiens-Old as he normally would, he thought he'd find someone else to help the man come up with the idea, and they could work on the invention together. It was unlikely that anyone would give this man an audience. He hesitated for some time, studying the people who passed by and did nothing to help.

Days went by, and still Michael had not seen anyone he felt was human enough to be the man's helper. No one had really dropped more than a few cents into the homeless man's bucket, except for this one woman, one that had come back for three days in a row, now.

She was beautiful, with her flowing red hair and hypnotic, grayish-blue eyes. She looked important, too, as she was with a couple of tall, strong men wearing sunglasses, walking on either side of her. He assumed they were bodyguards.

Each day for the next three days she came back, Michael saw her drop a $50 bill in his bucket while making sure not to be seen by the man. Michael smiled. He'd found the person that would help the man and his son. On the seventh day, Michael melded with the woman's body, and had her tell the bodyguards to wait behind for a minute as she talked to the homeless man.

While inside the woman's body, Michael had her explain to him how she'd seen him recently and how she was the one that had been giving him the $50 bills. She then explained how she wanted to help him more. The man smiled and asked, "What could I possibly offer a woman of your stature? Can't you see I'm a homeless, jobless man with a son I can barely take care of?"

She replied, "There's more to life than material things; I can just see something in you that is going to change the world. I don't know where these feelings come from, but I've gotten a good feeling every time I've seen you this week."

The man burst out in laughter, "How can *I* possibly do that? Society turned its back me, my boss firing me at the worst time in my life, right after my wife died. I have no desire to help change it now. I doubt I can make *anyone* feel good, not myself, not even my own son." The laughter quickly turned bitter.

Since a Modien can know instantly the entire life of the person they meld with, Michael understood how to help the man. He had the woman say in a reassuring voice, "I'm so sorry for your loss. I understand what it's like to lose a spouse. My husband passed away a few years ago, and I know the pain you're feeling. It will get better in time. Do you mind if I ask what it was that you did before you got fired? And I apologize if I'm being too forward."

He nodded, accepting her sympathy. "It's quite all right. I'm sorry for your loss, too. I was an engineer, designing airplanes. The company cut down the labor force with the new technologies of computers and satellites; they told me how they didn't need as many pilots or engineers anymore with the planes flying themselves, and I was laid off."

Michael thought for a minute, coming to the realization that giving the people of this planet all those technologies indirectly made this man, and probably countless others, homeless. He had an uneasy feeling again, like the one he had had after he thought he saw Amanda vanish into the crowd with Satan, but it was not as strong this time. "If there's an opposite of happy, this must be it," he thought to himself. Through the woman, he told the man how this was his lucky day, how she was an executive of one of the airlines in need of an engineer to design a new type of craft. She told the man she needed a craft that could travel into space, to other worlds and beyond, and how she needed his help.

The man laughed as he replied, "You're crazy, there's no way to...." Michael was taken aback by the man's response, forgetting that his idea has not yet been planted. He extended his hand outside the woman's body, still unseen by both, and into the head of the man, and sent a vivid picture of the spacecraft into the mind of the man. At that instant, the man stopped talking and smiled. "Even if it was possible to travel in space, what good would I be? I design airplanes. I don't know anything about space! All I can do is design the shape of the craft, and that's once I know *anything at all* about space, which I don't. No one does. All we've done is send satellites up there to help us communicate. No one has ever been in space."

"Nothing to worry about," Michael answered coyly while still inside the woman. "We'll just have to find out more about space for you to design a spacecraft then, won't we?"

They both smiled at each other. The man asked some more questions, and the woman convinced him to build this world's first spacecraft.

Michael exited the woman's body, smiling proudly at the feeling that he'd just done something new and different for this world and even for the way he gave Sapiens-Old ideas. "There; this planet has its invention for the day." He heard the A.T.M. tell him it had logged the day, the planet, the idea, the person it was given to, and the method into the mainframe of the Atomic Transference Machines System and into his Modien Essence Transmitter to be reloaded into his A.T.M. the next time he used it.

He decided to stay around for a while, blending in as one of the people closest to the project and making sure they did it right. He watched the two form and create the world's first spacecraft and the new industry of space travel for this planet. Months went by as they worked out the kinks of their invention with test after test. Each time, they designed a better version of the craft and got closer and closer to finishing their invention and making it safe enough for human travel.

The day finally came for them to unveil their creation. Michael looked on from the crowd. The two looked so happy, having created this momentous invention. They'd grown to love one another and had gotten married. He felt good knowing he had given the people of this world entirely new dreams to look forward to and goals to accomplish for a long time to come. He couldn't help but to think how God felt when he inspired someone. He wondered if it felt like this.

Satisfied, Michael told the A.T.M. to shut down, and within seconds all the work that he had done inside his universe was saved, and the universe collapsed into the small green speck of light once again, and then darkness. A second later, his Sphere of Life emerged from the little tube in the desk. Michael picked it up and it disappeared into his body to reattach itself to his Modien Essence Transmitter.

Michael was ecstatic and couldn't wait to tell Gabe. He left the A.T.M. room and headed for the break room, shouting for Gabe, but to no avail. Michael often forgot that he always finishes before anyone else. He had to wait to break the news to his best friend, and it felt like forever. When he finally saw him, he called, "Hey, Gabe! I've done something wonderful. I can't believe I haven't come up with this idea before!"

"What?"

"Well, normally I just give an idea to the Sapiens-Old that is the inventor, right?"

"Ummm, right...." Gabe said in wonderment, noticing how excited Michael was. "Well? Out with it! Don't leave me in suspense."

"Not only did I give the first one of my planets the gift of space travel, but I had TWO Sapiens-Old develop and share the idea—they helped each other! I couldn't believe how quickly the two of them worked to complete the first spacecraft for my universe. Usually, when I give the idea to just one person, it takes a while, but having the two cooperate in the making of the invention it went by twice as fast! I can't believe I haven't thought of this before. They even got married! It was amazing! "

"Wow, that's pretty impressive, buddy. How'd you come up with that?"

"I don't know, it just popped into my mind. I saw this homeless man, the first I'd ever seen, or at least the first one I've noticed. I wanted to help him so much I decided for him to be the inventor, but then I got the idea to give this man the idea with the help of this woman. It was the perfect match. It even turned out she was an executive in an airline company!"

Gabriel scratched his head, not understanding the full story, but he congratulated his friend all the same. "See, I told you, work was what you needed to cheer up. You haven't seemed yourself lately; I don't know what it is, but I know how wonderful you feel after you've given one of your Sapiens-Old a great idea."

"Heh, you know me pretty well, man. Thank you for suggesting that; I feel much better than I did before." They both sat in the break room, making something to snack on with the FFF. "Has Angelina designed your new house, yet?"

"Oh, yeah I forgot to tell you," he laughed. "She went all out with the decorations for the twins; in fact she even designed dual slides for the girls to slide down and get dressed at the same time. She's designed a lot of things made for two. It's almost like she designed one half of a house and copied it in two."

Michael laughed at the thought. "I'll have to check it out soon. How about Thursday? I don't think Marilyn is busy that night."

"Works for me. I'll let Angelina know. Hey, I meant to ask, how is Jacob? What'd he say about viruses?"

Michael remembered how Jacob said some people that are sick would be crazy, how the sickness was in their mind and they would see things that were not real, hear things that weren't there, so he decided not to share that with Gabriel. "We never really got into that; he's pretty sick himself, coughing uncontrollably. Lately, however, he just seems to not be himself, forgetting things, like my name. I never knew him to forget anything before. He also said how we're 'gravy' and in his day his kind had to work for the meat and potatoes."

"Gravy?" questioned Gabriel in disbelief.

Michael burst out laughing, remembering how his grandfather worded it and how bad his attempt at saying just was. "Yeah, gravy." He laughed some more. "Jacob said how us Modiens have life so easy with our control over things, like the weather and crops. How his kind would have to work hard for food and that the "gravy," as it were, was a luxury. Now it's all gravy … guess it means our lives are full of luxury."

"Ahhh, interesting. I never thought about that before. We really do have a remarkable life, don't we?"

"I guess we do.… Hey I have a great idea … how about you, Angelina, Max and the twins come with me, Marilyn, and Amanda to go and see Jacob Thursday instead? I'm sure he would be ecstatic about having us all there again. I think the last time he saw you two was when Max was born."

"Sounds like a wonderful plan, my friend."

"Great!" Michael sighed. "Guess I'll go see Daniel now. I don't look forward to it, though. I just don't understand why he purposefully tries to keep his distance from me. Even now, now that he has passed on. He just wants to go living around in his own heaven not wanting to spend much time with me. I can see it in his eyes after only a few minutes of me visiting him. He just wants to be in his perfect world."

"Why, don't you think it's perfect? Why would God and the Old say it was that way then? Don't you think if there wasn't a perfect system that they wouldn't have put it into place for the remainder of our existence?"

"I guess you're right, hard to doubt when you've met the Creator." He laughed at himself doubting God, especially having been in his presence for close to 340 years. "I don't know; I guess I am going to miss Jacob, is all. He's been acting weird lately, with the forgetting things … I know Sapiens-Old forget, and that he *is in fact* one, he just never acted this way before. I don't remember any member of the Old forgetting anything before, even if they were about to pass on."

Gabriel too tried to remember anyone ever forgetting anything and couldn't come up with an instance. "Well, let's hope his absentmindedness clears up soon." Gabe waited for a response from Michael after using such an archaic word.

"Absentmindedness … that's such an interesting word. Where'd you hear it? What's it mean?"

Gabriel smiled with excitement and explained his newly found word and what it meant. "I got it from the recent findings in the building of the underground transportation line from Aeon to Arcadia. That word, along with thousands of others from the past. It means someone is so lost in thought one does not know what is going on around them or what they're doing, even. I used it because it sounded to me like Jacob was thinking about his life and just forgot who he was talking to."

"Wow, that's quite a word, buddy. He was deep in thought about how long he'd lived and the changes he'd seen." Michael was extremely curious and couldn't imagine how Gabe received all those words from the excavation. "Where'd you get such an abundance of ancient words?"

"I won them in an auction. They're all put down on paper, bound together in what's called a dictionary…."

"An auction? How come I didn't hear about this? Awww man, I missed a chance to own actual artifacts from the times of the Old and before! Where was I?" Michael snarled down his s'mores and licked his fingers, trying to maintain some sense of dignity.

"I think you had to go to a dinner party with Marilyn that night. Something to do with her work, our race's breaking a deal with helping one of her planet's inhabitants from being exterminated in exchange for this new type of technology."

"Oh right, dang. I wish you could have gotten me a ticket for the raffle. But, I guess it is only fair the winners are the ones who actually attended the auction."

"Yeah, I'm sorry, man. Hey, you should see what Angelina got … you thought you were upset finding out you weren't there, I can't imagine how you're gonna feel hearing about what she got.…"

Michael glared at him for rubbing it in even more. "Yeah, yeah, I know, she was there for it, too, but I'm here for this!" He laughed and turned his watch so that it reflected the sun's rays directly into Gabriel's eyes.

"Hey, now," Gabriel lifted his arm up to shield his eyes. "I'll get you back, I always do."

"Oh, I count on it. I can always count on you, buddy. Even if it is for this childish game. Yet we can't seem to be able to stop playing it!" He laughed "Anyway, I'm off to see Daniel. I'm looking forward to Thursday, though."

"Oh, come now, you should know better than that. You can count on me for anything," said Gabriel, reinforcing the feelings of their life-long friendship.

"You're right, Gabe, you're right. Give my best to everyone."

Once again, Michael programmed his destination into the car and sat back, listening to more music while closing his eyes and remembering the look on Marilyn's face as she said yes to marrying him. How her eyes had sparkled and her face had lit up.

Then he remembered when Amanda was born, and the little twinkle in her eyes as she first looked up at him, and her first word, "Daddy. His whole life seemed to flash before his eyes, as if he was inside that new invention he saw not so long ago. How vivid it had all seemed. He wondered how such a machine could extract all those memories and make them seem so real, and yet so recent.

His car stopped. He saw the structures around the Building of Souls and realized that the trip had taken less time than before, and he got out of his car and watched it drive into the recycler.

Michael looked up the glistening blue Building of Souls and thought about the complexity that lay within. He walked slowly up the long row of sapphire steps, set in the shape of a semi-circle, and wondered if Jacob and his father could ever meet inside the Machine of Forever, once Jacob passed on, if the memories they had of each other would cross paths again and how that conversation would take place. He knew that others that had passed on had met each other, but Michael wondered if those two would even want to meet, seeing how different they were.

In fact, Michael never understood why his father wasn't as affectionate as Jacob was with him. How his father was always busy with the New Earth and trying to perfect it. "Granted," Michael thought, "he did help create the New Earth to pretty much what it was now by working closely with God. Maybe I should cut him some slack." A strong sense of pride began to well up in Michael, for his father and all his accomplishments. He thought that he was lucky to have such a father, one so dedicated to helping his fellow citizens, trying to make the world a better place, and establish new relations with other species across the universe. "Who else could have accomplished so much in his life?"

"Halt! Identify yourself," the Sentinel of Souls at the front desk demanded.

"I am Michael, son of Daniel and Jessica, grandson of Jacob the Old. I wish to see my father, Daniel." The robot scanned its files on Michael's DNA signature from the M.E.T. inside Michael's body.

"Michael, son of Daniel and Jessica, clearance is granted for access inside the Machine of Forever," the Sentinel of Souls allowed, lowering the electric field in front of the entrance to the Hallway of the Heavenly Coded.

Michael walked down the hallway and into the next available room. Once he was inside and the door shut behind him, the computer extracted Daniel's memories from the Ball of Essence, and trillions of lights of all colors began to glisten in the empty space in front of Michael, lighting up the room.

They formed what looked like a jungle to Michael, with thick foliage and a dense atmosphere. Huge stones created a room around him, making it pitch black and blocking out the noises of the animals and the tribesmen who were chanting somewhere in the distance. The feel of the place was eerily familiar but what or where it exactly was, escaped Michael's mind.

All of a sudden, light poured into the room through a wooden door that was opening slowly, and the sounds returned. Michael heard his father's voice shouting at people in some language he was not familiar with. As Daniel walked into the room, the animals fell silent and the chanting stopped.

Michael knew his father and all the effects were just programmed into Michael's vision inside the room from the Ball of Essence, but it seemed as real as the beat of his heart. "Michael, what brings you out my way? I was quite busy with something very important."

"Hi, Dad. It's nice to see you, too." Michael hugged him. "Nice place you have here. How are you?"

"Couldn't be better, son. I've figured something out that's been bothering me for quite some time and the solution is something I'm very proud of. It's never been done before in our illustrious Modified-Sapiens' history," Daniel boasted about the race he once was, forgetting that he had passed on and wasn't a Modien anymore. "I can't wait to see the outcome I'm expecting. But, enough talk, I need to relax. Let's go somewhere a little more soothing to my soul."

Daniel raised his arms from his sides and fanned them outward; instantly the massive stone room dissolved away, and then the jungle, too. Michael sighed as an open beach, waves crashing, appeared next to them.

"You loved the beach, didn't you Dad?" Michael smiled ruefully as he felt the wind in his hair, caught the scent of the salt air, and heard the roar of the tide.

Daniel smiled, then guffawed, "Couldn't do this in the New Earth before, now could we?" He rose in the sky and hovered just feet above Michael's head. As he looked down at his son, he pointed and lifted him up into the air, too. "What do you think about this? Pretty fun, isn't it?"

Michael had to admit it was. "It's incredible! How…? I thought…. Aren't we basically inside an A.T.M.? I thought we needed a craft to fly like this. We've never been able to fly like this before, not ever. Nobody has. How'd you figure this out?"

"Trust me, son, this is only the beginning. Follow me. I feel much better now." Daniel raced toward the sun, climbing higher and higher until he was out of Michael's sight.

After spending a couple of seconds thinking about whether he could actually chase his father down by flying, he started rising up into the air slowly. Michael realized that flying was as simple as thought. "Hey! Slow down! Where are you going? Come back!"

"Come on, Michael!" Daniel rose higher still. "I thought you had some curiosity and adventure in you." He soared right through the atmosphere and into the void of space.

They traveled for what seemed like forever to Michael, barely talking to each other, but that didn't even cross his mind, for he was far too busy enjoying being able to travel through space without the help of a craft. It even had this indescribable feeling, Michael noticed—it heightened his senses and imparted a warm feeling to his limbs and trunk. "Hey, Dad, how can we travel in the emptiness of space without being harmed by radiation? I feel so incredibly energetic! This is amazing."

"It's my heaven, Michael. It's my own Atomic Transference Machine. Don't you understand? All I needed was my imagination, and it happened. Some day you will understand. Ah, here we are. This place is really special to me, son. Follow me." Daniel started his descent through the planet's atmosphere, followed quickly by Michael.

They landed on what looked like an undeveloped planet, one with very few societies, as though it were a planet for a Modien who was just starting his own universe and this was his first attempt at creating a civilization. "These people aren't very technologically advanced at all. They look like they're barely through the Stone Age," Michael said out loud as they walked through a thick forest. It almost reminded Michael of his very first planet. A huge, pyramid-looking building rose above the rest of the city, which had been carved out of the dense surroundings to dominate the landscape. "It's all so familiar," he blurted out. Daniel said nothing but continued walking into the crowded center of this Stone Age-looking primitive city.

Everyone recognized Daniel and those closest to him started to bow down in homage as the rest cheered. They offered up their goods to him and Michael, making sure not to look directly at Daniel's face. Daniel talked to them in their native language, and they stood up, looking at each other, wondering what he would do next.

Whatever Daniel said prompted some of the people to run and get two huge, elaborately ornate chairs connected to platforms. Daniel motioned for Michael to take one as he mounted the other. The people carried them off to the biggest pyramid in the city.

"Hey, Dad... What's going on here?"

"What does it look like, Michael?"

Michael was affronted by his tone of voice, one of arrogance and condescension. It reminded him of some of the Sapiens-Old on the planets he had in his universe, how they would talk down to their subordinates. It looked like his own father was acting like a god, something Modiens were told never to do while working inside their universes. He figured that the same didn't apply to those that have passed on and he answered, "Looks like you're having quite a good time, actually."

"I am, indeed. I don't want to say it's the best time in my life, because that wouldn't fit, now would it? However, I must say that passing on has been quite an experience, and that I've actually learned new things when I thought I wouldn't."

As Michael listened to his father, a woman with an older man walked up through the crowd and kept pace with them, talking to Daniel. He assumed the older man was the woman's father. Upon a closer look at this woman, he realized that she looked almost exactly like his mother, Jessica, from his father's descriptions of her and the images he'd seen in the archives. She had long red hair with greyish-green eyes and pale skin.

The men carrying Michael and Daniel lowered them down at the top of one pyramid, just outside a lavish room filled with ornate decorations and food. There were strange figures lined up on either side of the entrance, figures carved out of stone, people, but they weren't in grand or guard-type. These people looked frightened.

The couple that had been walking next to them stopped next to Daniel. He put his arm around the woman's shoulders and spoke to her in a foreign language. It reminded Michael of an ancient dialect from somewhere, but he couldn't put his finger on it. Everyone in the crowd cheered and celebrated in honor of their god's return.

Daniel looked over at Michael. "Michael, my son, I'm having a glorious time indeed," he bellowed. "I should have thought of this long ago," he continued. "It only came to me recently, though, like a thunderbolt. Not that I wasn't having fun before, but it just felt like something was missing, and now I've found that something. Anyway, what is new on the Outside? How is Amanda? You're going to bring her to me again soon, aren't you? Isn't she going to have her first Big Bang soon?"

"Yup, not too long now. Wow, seems like only yesterday she was even born. You were right—time flies when you're having fun. I finally understand what you meant by that when you said it when she was born. How one day I'd look back and realize it went by so fast!" Michael looked around at the people staring at them as they walked to the thrones built for Daniel inside the room of the pyramid palace. "Can these people understand us?"

"Nope, they sure as Hell can't," Daniel smirked.

Again, Michael was taken aback, not only by his father's tone, but by what he said. He'd never heard him say that word before. He's never heard *anyone* say "Hell" outside of the teachers talking about it in school. He remembered them saying that "Hell" wasn't an actual physical place, that it was a state of mind, or consciousness. He also remembers hearing that the person creates the state of mind that's filled with all the fears and horrors they've learned of or experienced in their lives. And when Homo sapiens died, the ones that kept those fears in their minds would have that negative energy carry over into their afterlife until they learned to deal with it over time. The teachers also explained how Satan had invented the concept of evil just to prove a point with God. They never said what that point was, since Satan admitted defeat upon the Great Battle of Souls of the human race, and was kept in silence once he was encaged.

Michael decided to play along. He laughed, "Well, good. I sure as *Hell* don't want them to tell on us." Michael looked over at Daniel and they both started laughing.

Then the crowd inside the gigantic room inside the palace laughed nervously, not really knowing why their god was laughing to begin with, but they had learned to do whatever Daniel did or ordered them to for fear of some sort of punishment.

Michael just stood there, not knowing how to react at all. He assumed this was the norm. He'd never experienced being treated in such a way, as a god, being carried around, pandered to, and revered by the masses. He figured what his father was doing, was *what gods do*, displaying their power but trying to be one with the people at the same time. Michael thought that if God had to deal with this type of behavior from his followers at one point in time, that seeing his father in the same circumstances wasn't so bad after all. He decided to enjoy this visit with his father, because most visits weren't nearly as pleasant as this one was shaping up to be.

"So, my child, my creation … what can I do for you? I know you see Jacob more than I. I forgive you for that, though, you can relate to him more than to me. I see this now."

Flabbergasted, Michael asked, "How do you know I see him more?"

"Well, even though I have passed on, I still have connections on the outside. Some even see me more often than you do, maybe as often as you go and see Jacob, but I'm not bitter toward you or him. He was around more than I was, especially during those early years…. So was Clarice. It was a good thing; it was something you needed that I couldn't give you at the time. Not because I didn't want to, but because I didn't realize what I had." Daniel looked down. Then, as quickly as lightning bursts through the air, he raised his arm up, and a brilliant golden light struck one of the people inside the room, turning him into stone, suddenly and without warning. The rest of the people gasped, but quickly continued eating their dinner and talking to each other as if nothing had happened. They'd seen this before, feeling lucky that it was not they who had been turned to stone. Daniel let out a laugh and looked over at Michael. "Not to worry, Michael … this isn't real, remember? They don't exist. This is the universe I had when I was alive. Look here." He picked out a child from the room, a sick child, and he lifted the young boy up above his head and the rest of the people, just like he'd lifted Michael off the beach. The crowd looked on nervously. Michael could see the people's expressions of fear and uncertainty. He was stunned by his fathers' actions.

"This poor, young boy is dying of cancer," Daniel explained to Michael. "I noticed him coughing uncontrollably once during my many journeys to this village in recent months. It makes me so happy to be able to help beings like this poor boy, here. Watch." He brought the child between him and Michael and looked out over the crowd. "This, this is my heaven.…" He put his hand *into* the chest of the little boy, who was screaming in fright now, making the crowd grow ever more nervous as they watched, helplessly. He pulled his hand out of the screaming child, and within his clenched fist was a blackened, grisly piece of flesh, still dripping with blood and pus. A tumor. Daniel showed it to Michael, and then lifted it up to the crowd. Daniel lowered his other hand and, in the same motion, placed the gasping boy back on the ground. The young boy had stopped screaming and coughing. He smiled an angelic smile, and hugged Daniel. Everyone went wild, cheering and calling out his name in an ancient dialect that Michael still couldn't quite place. Daniel looked up at Michael while on one knee. "So, what do you think, son?"

"Pretty amazing, Dad. I'm so glad you've adapted to passing on so well. For a while, there, it seemed you didn't like it. I'm glad you saved that boy's life from that sickness, and I was wondering, since you brought it up—" Michael didn't even have time to finish.

"Oh, I've adapted, all right, Michael, and soon so will everyone else. But, I'm sorry I interrupted you. Please go on."

"Well, I was just wondering what you remember of "colds" and "viruses." Did your dad ever talk about them? You know, in the time of the Old?"

Daniel thought to himself, then answered carefully, "He told me that they are very contagious sometimes and what caused the symptoms would change or mutate over time. So whatever infection a being had, the disease itself would adapt to vaccinations, grow stronger and more resistant to the antidotes developed to fight them. Some viruses were so deadly to the Old and the Sapiens-Old they would catch whatever it was and die within days. Good thing we worked with God to eliminate those. Us Modiens—excuse me, *you* Modiens, such as I *was*, will never have to worry about those kinds of viruses and colds. Speaking of which, I heard Jacob is sick; how is he?"

Puzzled as to how he would know that, Michael didn't answer right away.

"Michael? Just like you, always daydreaming. Even when you were a kid you'd daydream all the time…. Michael!" Daniel clapped his hands in front of his child, who was off somewhere in his mind, wandering.

"Oh, sorry! I was just noticing how this woman looks like Mom, or at least what I imagine what she'd look like from what I know. This whole place seems so familiar, actually. Anyway, what did you say to the people earlier that made them cheer so much when this old man and woman came?" Michael pointed to the woman's father, who stood up straight, smiled and bowed his head to Michael. Michael smiled back and bowed. "When did you two meet? How did you find this place?"

"This, my boy, is going to be my new wife. The reason she looks like your mother is that I've spent what seems like an eternity looking for another woman that could replace the wife I lost."

"I remember, Dad. You didn't seem yourself after she passed on, or at least that's what Jacob told me. He's coughing an awful lot, Dad. Is he going to be okay?"

"He'll be fine, Michael, trust me. Even he will pass on; he'll be in *Heaven*, right? I mean, look at me. I'm doing all right. Don't you think?"

"Well, yeah…. It's just … I never saw him this way before. He is so sick, and he even said he was dying. I've never really seen anyone die before."

"Michael, he is a Homo sapiens; they get sick."

Again his tone went askew, sounding almost like sarcasm from the Sapiens-Old in Michael's universe. Being far too sad about Jacob's illness to question his fathers' tone, he answered, "Yes, I suppose he is, and I suppose they do get sick and die."

"I'm sorry, my boy, but it's a part of life. I didn't think I'd wind up here…." Daniel stopped talking, and looked back at all he had done to help God and the Old and the entire Modien race as a whole.

"I remember how I was the first Modien ever and all the requests that were asked of me by the Old. I remember their ideas of what *exactly* a Modien could and couldn't do. How I spent what seemed like forever being modified; time and time again going through the Olds' idea of the perfect species to replace their own kind. How I was to be the next step in the human race's history and those that were made after me. I felt pride knowing all this hard work would pay off; I felt my help was going to be the staple for the new Modified-Sapiens species. With my input, we were going to be the smartest and most responsible species ever to walk on the face of the Earth, and I loved the fact I was the very first one of our kind."

He laughed. "I remember when the Old thought that Modiens should be able to defy gravity and fly around to wherever they want at a moment's notice, and how I took off for the first time and couldn't stop ascending. I kept going higher and higher until God himself had to be told to come and stop me before reaching the atmosphere, where I'd be destroyed by the radiation. The idea of flight was scratched soon after.

"Then the Old thought that Modiens shouldn't get dirty. No matter how I tried to stay clean, dirt still accumulated upon my body. It turned out this was because as I moved, all the trillions of nano-bots created static electricity, and picked up dust and dirt no matter what I did to try to avoid it. Some of the Old were disappointed, while others didn't mind the idea of bathing still being a part of the Modien experience. As it turns out, I, like the rest of us Modiens, love showers. You know that feeling, Michael; the feeling of water falling through your entire body, cleaning each particle of our nano-bots. It really creates a sensation that is indescribable to the Old and their understanding of feelings."

Michael thought to himself how fascinating his kind really was, how much more capable they were of enjoying everything they encountered compared to his grandfather and the rest of the Old. He sat there listening to his father tell a tale he'd never told before, and he wondered why. Before now, when asked, Daniel would just smile and tell him how it was a magical and heartbreaking experience, and that was all he'd say.

Daniel continued, "One time, the Old got rid of my atom-by-atom Modien body completely and went with a metal skeleton with a fleshy exterior. That didn't work out well at all; even I knew that was a bad idea, but I went along with it anyway.

"I also didn't like the idea of my thoughts being trapped inside a single microchip. Even though I still had all the knowledge I was given, it felt like my thinking was more confined somehow … it didn't feel natural. I liked the way my atom-by-atom Modien body felt, where all the information was held within each individual nano-bot and thoughts were able to flow freely throughout my body. I never could have imagined something like that to be possible, how my thoughts felt constricted inside a single microchip." He stopped talking and wondered if he was the only Modien that would ever know the difference between the two types of bodies.

"I also missed the feeling of the wind moving over my entire body, which consisted of trillions of nano-bots. Each one was capable of feeling the wind, unlike the exposed skin of this metal hunk of junk I was trapped inside. So God and the Old went back to the Modified-Sapiens model where all the nano-bots were able to move from one to another and free-flowing thought and sensation were once again present. I was very pleased indeed.

"I felt like I'd live forever and be revered forever. After all, I was, in fact, the Olds' pride and joy. But, better still, I was God's pride and joy. Yes, I felt as though I was God's right-hand man, and that it was going to be the two of us forever.

"Those were the best days of my life. I had this brand new world with which to start a brand new society, and a brand new wife to top it all off. I remember thinking that if this was only New Earth and life is so amazing now, imagine what the other Modiens will think when they pass on. I even remember thinking to myself how I probably won't ever experience that sensation of an afterlife. Why would God *kill* the first Modien? And I assumed I wouldn't pass on. Boy was I wrong.

"For decades, I'd invent modes of transportation that were safe for the environment and huge buildings that dwarfed anything built before. I'd design skyscrapers that would literally scrape the edge of the atmosphere, and were stunning to look at for hundreds of miles around. There are even designs of mine still around today, the ones that mimic mountain chains, that have created different weather patterns in parts of the world that were once uninhabitable, making that part of the world capable of growing vital crops to sustain life. This was before a Modien developed the Weather Maker, the device that is capable of changing the weather in a backyard or an entire region.

"I created art, music, and plays for the theater that are still mimicked in some fashion by Modiens to this day. I created some of the most beautiful pieces of music that made the Old fall to their knees and beg for more while, at the same time, inspiring other Modiens to try to do the same.

"There are still sides of entire buildings where I've painted scenes that 'Can move the dead,' as one member of the Old put it. Beings from all around the galaxy and beyond would make special trips just to see my work. I had it all then, and I didn't even realize it."

In thinking about his early life with dear admiration, he smiled broadly. He realized that for the briefest of moments the entire universe was paying attention to him, something he not only did not see, but failed to enjoy. "No longer will I take for granted what I once did; I will have my time in the light again, once I reveal myself to the world as someone who's defied death. I will tell them that I can bring their loved ones back from death, too, so that they can enjoy their presence without having to go to the Building of Souls. I will have the admiration of everyone once again."

Daniel shook his head from deep thought. "Michael, do you still love me? I have these feelings lately that you somehow resent me."

"Resent you? For what reason would I resent you? I will always love you, Dad."

"I just feel like I wasn't around enough for you. Funny, isn't it? Here I am, eons away from where I started, yet it still feels like yesterday when my existence first came to be. I'm so happy you love me still, and forever will. It will make things much easier for me from now on." Daniel looked at Michael and pulled him in for a hug. He held his son's face, looking at him closely. "Now, enough of this … I didn't bring you here for this. This is going to be a celebration! Tonight we will throw a feast like no other, for tomorrow I will marry again!"

Michael smiled and put up his hands on top of his father's. He then raised the right hand into the air and spoke to the others in their native tongue, telling the others to cheer for his father and for his new bride-to-be.

Daniel looked back over at him curiously, but knew it didn't take much for Michael to pick up on anything he didn't know. He's always known Michael was exceptionally smart, even for a Modien. He told the people that this was a new time for them; they will rise up as one and will enjoy the benefits of life that he has, and how no one will ever know pain or suffering again. He told them how grateful he was to them for letting him into their society, and for allowing him to marry this beautiful woman of theirs. Everyone jumped in the air, zealously rooting for their new god, one who has given them health and wealth already beyond what they ever knew. Since his arrival, they had risen in power and wealth among the other tribes in the area, and had become a huge force in the region. For all this, they loved their new god and would die for him.

Michael was enjoying his time with his father for once; he'd never seem him this happy before. He wondered what his heaven would be like once he entered the Machine of Forever. "Father," Michael said in Modien, which was much like the ancient language of English, and, since most of the Old spoke it, it became the official language of the Modien race, all of the languages that weren't English still survives though, there's some that speak it for fun and others to preserve them. "Do you know how Grandpa got a cold to begin with? I thought colds were eradicated from the New Earth after the Switch. I mean, the nanos have pretty much taken care of any disease since they were invented."

"Ah, son, I don't know anything anymore; I'm just a man in love again. Besides, what can I do? I'm bound for eternity in here. I don't understand why the nanos haven't healed Jacob yet, though … whatever illness he has must be something new, since they haven't got whatever it is on record yet or they would have identified it as something harmful and cured him. That's just what the nanos do."

"I … I know that death is just a part of life; when I lost you I felt just as bad as I do now, if not worse. This time it's different, though. I mean, Jacob is sick. I've never seen anyone die from a sickness before." Michael put his head in his hands and shook it side to side.

Daniel sat down with a puzzled look on his face. "I had a feeling, but I wasn't sure. You hardly see me in here anymore, you see Jacob more. It makes everything feel so...." He paused again, speechless for a few seconds. Then, without warning, he raised his arm and pointed it at the man he had turned to stone earlier. Another bolt shot from the tip of his finger, and the man turned back from stone, looking around, not knowing what happened to him. Daniel told everyone to prepare for the feast tonight with his son, and everyone cheered for him and their god, running out of the room laughing and talking. "Stay with me, at least for the feast, and then tomorrow you can leave. It would mean so much to me."

Michael agreed and together they walked over to Daniel's bride. "Michael, this is Manaba," Daniel said, appraising her unabashedly. The woman really did look like his mother. Michael was amazed at how this woman knew so much about the way the planet worked, how she was going to be the tribe's queen once her father died. She knew that her father's ways of keeping a balance with nature were important, and planned to continue his legacy. Michael was impressed with her. He felt comfortable with her, as though he'd known her his entire life. They all enjoyed the celebration that night and feasted upon some of the best-tasting food Michael had ever eaten. There was wild boar so succulent it fell off the bone and melted in Michael's mouth, and strange vegetables that were sweet and sour at the same time. They drank a fermented concoction made from a fruit that reminded him of a strawberry and banana at the same time.

The next day, as the Sapiens-Old were beginning to wake up, Daniel and Michael were still talking from the night before. This was the most time he had spent with his father, ever. Michael learned so much about him and the times before he was born, and how Daniel would come up with the ideas for all his inventions; he never realized what a gentle soul his father had, and he wondered how it had taken all this time to find these things out.

"Michael, remember this moment," Daniel begged of his son. "Remember how happy we are now and how I feel this new life is best for me. Just remember. And bring Amanda by soon; I miss her. She sort of reminds me of you at that age."

"I will, Dad. She'll be excited to see you again, too, I'm sure. I'd better get back now. I'm sure Marilyn is wondering what I found out about viruses. She's worried about Jacob, too; we all are."

"Yes, go now. You know where to find me." They all raised a glass to Michael, and Daniel told Michael to be careful, not to catch Jacob's cold. "I love you, son. I always will." He and his fiancée hugged Michael, and they all prepared for his departure.

As quickly as he could think about how to leave, Michael found himself back inside the empty room inside the Building of Souls. He headed outside, and didn't understand why it was dark. "I was only gone five minutes. How could it be dark? Usually the visits in the Machine of Forever only took five minutes of real time, just like at work with the A.T.M. He couldn't imagine what had happened to the rest of the time. A few hours must have passed, at least. How strange! He was thinking he'd better get home to Marilyn—she must be worried something terrible. Weird.

As Michael got into his car, another vision pierced into his mind, this time of Amanda and Daniel running off through a dense forest. In the vision, Michael screamed out, "No! She needs me, I need to save her. She needs me, she needs me!" A brilliant white light flashed over his eyes, and again, he was back on his way home.

What the hell was going on with him? He'd been growing more and more worried as the frequency of the visions increased and he still had no idea what was causing them, or what to do. He supposed it was time to stop ignoring the fact they were happening. The car's stereo started playing another ancient song that had survived, Radiohead's "Creep." Michael was amazed by how often, of the countless hours of songs he had in his collection, that just the right song for an occasion seemed to play without him choosing it. He had never really understood the meaning of this particular song before; he could never get on the same wavelength as those who wrote it over 1,000 years before. It always made him feel good, though; it gave him hope and made him feel he wasn't alone. Then the images of the vision of Daniel running away with Amanda came back; they frightened him. As the car pulled up to his building, he shook off the heebie-jeebies again, and composed himself before going inside. He smiled at the familiar surroundings of home.

"Michael! Where have you been?" Marilyn rushed up to him in frenzy. "I thought you were going to see Jacob and Daniel today." She wrapped her arms around him and gave him a big hug.

"I … I did I didn't realize it would take so long. I'm sorry. I didn't mean to make you worry. I guess I lost track of time." He hugged her back and kissed her forehead. "Hey. I'll make it up to you. Let's go somewhere, all of us. Amanda, have any suggestions?"

"Oh, oh! How about Disney Universe," asked Amanda. The Modiens had rebuilt Disney World after the Apocalypse as a tribute to the lighthearted spirit of the human race. Only this one was huge; it basically covered the entire peninsula of what was the state of Florida during the time of the Old. "Please, Daddy? Pretty please!"

Michael laughed, delighted by his daughter's enthusiasm. Talk about "gravy!" I guess even kids who seemingly had it all could still get excited about certain things. "Okay, okay, we'll go. I do like the new slides they've built."

"New slides? Oh Daddy, you're so old fashioned. They're as old as old is! They were one of the first rides when they built Disney Universe!"

"I know, sweetie, but you know me with things from the time of the Old, they fascinate me. Besides, if they were some of the first rides to be rebuilt, doesn't that mean people missed them?"

"Oh, yeah," she thought about him always eating s'mores, and the car he drove. "Well, okay, we can go on them, but after we go to Epcot. It's my favorite."

"Good thing this is a long weekend," Michael said. "I don't want to lose any of my planets because I spent prime idea-giving time on Disney! Sound good, baby?" Michael asked Marilyn.

She looked back at him and smiled. "Oh yeah! I love the roller coasters." She wrapped her arms around Michael's neck and gave him a kiss.

"Roller coasters, yes! That's what I'm talking about, Mom! I can't wait to go on Space Mountain! I always think the shield won't come up to protect us from the vacuum and radiation of space, but just at the last nano-second, it appears," Amanda exclaimed with glee in anticipation.

They arranged for Brody to go stay at Gabriel and Angelina's house, and headed off to the travel center to spend the next couple of days at Disney Universe.

"Hey, Daddy, did Great Grandpa Jacob ever go to the original Disney World?"

"I think so, sweetie; I remember him saying he went there once with his girlfriend when he was young."

"Wow, really? What'd he say? What were the rides like? Were they anything like they are today?" Were Mickey Mouse and Goofy around back then? Is it true Walt Disney is still frozen?"

Michael laughed at the plethora of questions coming from his daughter. "You're so inquisitive, darling! That's one of the things I love most about you. Wow, there were quite a few questions there. Let's see. I remember him saying the rides were amazing, even back then, but that they weren't anything like they are now."

"Like *how*, did he say?"

"Well, he did say how the rollercoasters weren't even close to the size of the ones we have now, and they weren't nearly as intricate, either. And Mickey and Goofy have been around for a very long time, and Mickey was the very first character in Disney. Did you know Mickey was originally named Mortimer?"

"Really? No, I didn't know that! Wow, so what was Goofy's original name?"

"Dippy Dog," answered Michael.

"Dippy Dog, huh? Who thought of that? I like Goofy better."

"Me too, darling. Now, let's go, shall we?"

"You bet, Daddy. Ready, Mommy?"

Marilyn smiled. "Yes, dear. I can't wait for 'It's A Nano-World after All!' That's another one of my favorites!."

After they landed the jump off the roof of their building, they walked to the corner travel center. Amanda asked, "Hey, Dad, since the rides are so much bigger now than they were when Great Grandpa Jacob went there, how big was Disney Universe back then?"

"Well, it was quite big, actually, but it's nothing compared to today. Even though most of what was Florida is underwater now, the rest is Disney Universe, all the way up to a city that was called Atlanta, and all the way East to the Atlantic Ocean."

"Wow! That's pretty big! Is it just to fit all the rides?"

"No, sweetie, they also have a huge natural forest that helps preserve countless species both from the time of the Old and ones we have made. In fact, Disney Universe works with the keepers of the Forest of the Old, where all the animals of the times of the Old that survived are kept."

"Why is that, though, Daddy?"

"Well, the Forest of the Old starts along the area where Disney World ended; the land was unused by Disney Universe at the time and they wanted to pay their respects to the Old."

"That's neat. I wonder what will happen once all the members of the Old have passed on, though."

Michael had never thought about that, and thinks not many have, actually; leave it to Amanda to come up with such a question. "Not sure, sweetheart, but let's go inside and go through the 'It's a Nano-World after All' ride."

"Okay, Daddy. This is going to be fun! Come on, Mommy!" Amanda ran off ahead of them, shouting back for them to hurry up.

"Michael," Marilyn asked in a worried tone, "is everything all right, baby? You don't seem yourself lately. You seem distracted."

"I do?" Michael answered. "I haven't noticed me being any different, let alone distracted. I have everything in my life I could possibly want. What made you ask that?"

"I don't know, you just seem a little off since I've been home. I know you're worried about Jacob and all, but it seems like there is something else."

Michael kissed her forehead and ran his fingers through her long, dark brown hair, not wanting to share the horrible visions with her yet. "Everything is fine, baby; I promise. Come on, it's your turn to get shrunk. "

Marilyn smiled in relief. "All right, sweetheart, if you say so." With that, they climbed into a little craft on the platform a few steps above them, and a bright orange light fired like a laser from a dish. Instantly they were shrunk to the size of a handful of atoms and carried off into the ride. "Here's the first room," Marilyn exclaimed as they were whisked through a vein from one of the Olds' species, watching blood cells knock around each other and hit the walls of the vein. A few seconds went by and they were in front of what looked like the heart, and just as they were about to pass through it, the scenery changed to that of huge billowy clouds in a bright blue sky.

Now they were the size of a tiny spore of bacteria, floating along the breezes of the Earth; the view was stunning. They saw eagles flying next to them, and their prey, and when one swooped down to catch a rabbit, their view was that of the eagle racing down toward the ground. They soared up into the sky with the eagle, the rabbit in its clutches, swerving to avoid some rainclouds. Droplets began to fall all around them, huge as air balloons. One hit them, and they fell to the ground inside the rain drop, splashing into a huge lake and bobbing.

They giggled with exhilaration, floating for a few seconds. After feeling a strange pulling sensation, they realized they were a part of a huge sequoia tree that was growing up hundreds of feet into the air. They began to laugh again as they got tickled by all the animals and insects running over them, then they were stunned into silence by the warmth of the sun on their faces. The view of the treetops was overwhelming as their tree rose above the rest. The crisp, clean air rushing past and through them brought them to tears; they'd never before felt the sensation of growing, growing tall and majestic in the open. Finally, they landed on a field where people were playing a game; they could see a small white ball sailing toward them, landing just behind them, being chased by a player. A calming silver light, like that of the full moon, enveloped them. The ride was over; their bodies were back to normal. They looked at each other for a few minutes, not needing to speak.

Then: the slides! They started miles in the air, streaming through different environments built around them. Michael loved this one slide that started with a chilly artic climate. "Come on!" he said, but he could tell that the girls would rather sit this one out. "Suit yourselves! See you on the other sideeeeeee!!!!! He reveled in the crisp, cold air and the frolicking, fighting polar bear cubs. Farther down, going through a sultry jungle stage, he heard the squawks of the birds and the chirps of the insects along with oppression of the dense, thick atmosphere. Finally, Michael whisked through a desert, creating a sand storm behind him as he hurdled downward. He glided just inches above the barren sand dunes that stretched for miles upon miles, until he saw an oasis and a plethora of animals all sharing the watering hole. The slide tore through the small pool of the oasis, refreshing Michael after the hot, dry desert. He landed at the bottom, dripping, with a huge smile on his face.

"How was it, Dad? Did we miss anything???"

"You'll have to see for yourselves!" Michael teased.

"Okay, okay," Amanda said. "But first, the roller coasters!"

The content parents watched as Amanda raced off to the nearest one, dodging Disney-goers as she went. The coaster sent her through incredible scenes: she raced behind a comet's tail, watching the glittering pieces of its head fall off and sail around her, disappearing into the darkness of space behind her. Torrents of wind rushed through her as her car barreled through the funnel of a tornado. Suddenly quiet as a tomb, she was gliding over the ocean floor, dolphins and sea turtles, which she'd only seen on her vidscreen at home, nipping playfully at her knees and elbows. She loved this one; every time she'd been on it, the scenery had changed so she'd never had the same experience twice.

"That really is my favorite!" shouted the girl breathlessly, as she ran back to her waiting parents. They began to walk on through the immense park. "Sea turtles, comets oh! Epcot! My favorite!" Amanda shouted with glee; her mom and dad rolled their eyes at each other. Amanda, oblivious, went on. "Remember last time? The black hole? Hey, Dad, what do you think it is this time? Do you think it's going to be black holes again, or do you think they will try to recreate the past again? How come we waited to go to Epcot? We always wait, when I always want to come here first."

Michael laughed, "I know, angel, but every time we go to Epcot, we're here for the rest of our time. And you always say it's worth the wait. We'll just have to see what Epcot has to offer, now won't we? Besides, ever hear of the expression, 'save the best for last'?"

"Yeah, yeah," she giggled, "I hope it's something new! I always love new things!"

As they got to the entrance, they saw that the feature was parallel universes. The three of them were awestruck as they entered the ride. Then, as they exit, they are astonished beyond belief at what they just experienced.

"Words can't describe that … I'm speechless," exclaimed Marilyn.

"Me neither! I never knew things could ever be so different.… What'd you think, Amanda? Wasn't it worth the wait?"

She stood there with her jaw hanging, and just smiled widely, hugging them both.

Michael laughed. "I think she liked it, too."

"Why don't we get something to eat. I made us reservations at the Maze of Inter-dimensional Aliment."

"Ya, ya!" cried Amanda. "I love eating at M.I.A.! Not only is the food great, but the mazes are always different!"

"Sure," Marilyn agreed. "I always have a great time there."

"Did everyone have a good time?" asked Michael.

"Again, again," demanded Amanda.

"No, sweetheart, we'll come again," Marilyn told her.

"Awww, Mom! One more ride? Pretty please?"

"Sorry, angel. I promise we will come back soon; let's go eat now. Not only am I hungry, you have to study some more, and your father and I have to talk alone."

"Awww ... okay, Mom. I can't wait to come back again, though! We'll have more fun then, I guess. Let's go home. I'm starving."

After leaving Disney Universe, Michael, Marilyn, and Amanda went back to Aeon. They waited in line to confirm their registration to participate in the Maze of Inter-dimensional Aliment events for the night.

While waiting in line, Amanda heard a boy behind her ask his father what it would be like, and before the father could answer Amanda said in excitement, "This is one of the best rides outside of Disney Universe! Every time I have come to eat here, the mazes have all been different."

"Wow, coolacious," exclaimed the boy. "What else?"

"Well, first off, the whole audience surrounds the entire maze and can see all the action through a special glass that allows them to see the teams jump backward and forward in time."

"You're kidding! You mean that's true? That's so awesome! So you mean, while we're eating, we can travel back to like when the dinosaurs were on the Earth?"

Amanda giggled. "No, not that I know of, we can't go back that far in time, at least not here. But, we can go into the future and see how to solve a puzzle, or what we might have to do next to move forward in the maze."

The young boy looked up at Amanda in awe. "So what does time travel feel like?"

Smiling and looking back down at him, she said, "That's something you will just have to feel for yourself. But, trust me, you will like it; it's a feeling that nothing can compare to. It gives me chills just thinking about the fact that I'm going to have it soon."

"So how does a team win?"

"Well, that has always changed, just like how I've never played the same maze twice. Most of the game involves solving something to unlock the time warp button, or building something to weigh down a platform so it sinks underneath the structure, and when it sinks far enough, it triggers another clue or a time warp button, or who knows it could shoot out food. That's the best thing about the Maze of Inter-dimensional Aliment, I've been here two dozen times and each time the maze was completely different."

"Wow! How do they make each maze so different?"

Again Amanda smiled. "That's another cool part about M.I.A.; every team that wins can design a maze for the following week. So the winners create the next maze and they can watch the two teams work their way through and finish. Some mazes I've been in look like actual mazes with a path to the finish, others I've walked upside-down in and underwater. You never know what the designers have thought of on how to create the maze."

"I can't wait to play! Have you ever won before?"

"Oh, yes. I've won 16 times out of 24."

"That's a great average. You must be very smart."

"Well, I am, but so is my family. I can't win on my own; no one can. I misspoke earlier when I said 'I've won.' I meant…"

The boy smiled. "I know what you meant; that's still a great average, though. Do you play random teams or others that you already know?"

"Mostly we play our best friends. We've played them 16 times and won eight times and lost eight times. In fact, we haven't lost to any other families at all."

"Wowzinga," the boy said in amazement. "Looks like it's your turn to register," he pointed to the lectern.

"Thank you! And good luck tonight." Amanda put her hand up for a high-five and the boy obliged.

"Thanks! Good luck to you, too. I sure hope we don't face you tonight," the boy said with a nervous laugh.

"Well, if we do face off with each other, I'll be sure to try and take it easy on you. Take care, lil' guy. Hurry. Daddy! I can't wait!"

"Yes, darling. Patience, though." Michael patted her head then talked to the woman behind the counter. "We have a seven-thirty reservation."

"Certainly, sir. Would you please step in here so we can identify you all?" The woman pointed to a small doorway where scanners read their M.E.T., allowing the system to determine their DNA for entrance to the event.

As the three of them walked through the entrance to meet the other team, they are told the rules for the night by the announcer through the loudspeakers. "Ladies and gentlemen, those participating in tonight's event and to all that are watching, per the design of last week's winners, Benjamin, his wife Celeste, and their children Paul and Erica, there will be three different time warps scattered over the mountain the participants must climb in tonight's maze.

"The first time warp is activated once a single player on each team reaches the top of this plateau first." Spotlights shine down on the top of the plateau overhead, specifically over the button itself, and the audience cheers. "Once a player reaches the top and pushes the button, the remaining players are thrust ahead thirty seconds into the future to reconstruct a bridge from raw materials, in order to cross the lava lake, while the first player remains thirty seconds in the past.

Building the bridge will unlock a door for the first player to rejoin the group thirty seconds into the future, plus however long it took them to build the bridge, allowing the whole team to move onward in the maze.

"The teams must then cross a molten lake of lava using the bridge they just built, in order to activate the second time warp. How they move the bridge over the lake will be up to the team. There are several ways to place the bridge into position across the lake of lava, each requiring the teams to use items made available to them.

"Each of the items available to move the bridge has a different time price allotted to it, and none of the items have the same amount of time added to the overall score of the team after they finish. The more a team uses the same item, the more time is charged for that usage. The items include levers that are large enough to pivot the bridge across the lake; a levitation device to move the bridge a certain length for each usage; and a crane that charges for a one-time usage, but has a larger penalty to use than the others, or may take more overall time to operate. The overall time added to each team is determined by the items they use and how often they use them.

"After the teams reach the other side of the lava lake and push the second time-warp button, they are sent ahead in time again, two minutes into the future. There they will see the results of the completion of the next obstacle they face, building a pathway to the finish line, but they will not see how they put it together, or who will win. They will only see what the finished pathway looks like, and where it begins. From this they will have to figure out how they made it.

"Once the teams find the place to build the pathway to the finish line, they will have to push the third time warp button; they will then be transported 1 minute and 59 seconds backward in time to just after they crossed over the bridge. There they will see a series of numbers and determine which number comes next in the sequence and then determine the prime for that number. They will repeat that step another time and then use those two prime numbers as the number of pieces needed to build the pathway to reach the top of the mountain and the finish line. For example, a team has two prime numbers of 11 and 17; they will have to use 11 pieces of about 27 feet tall and 17 pieces of about 17 feet tall each. While each team will have a different number of pieces to use in the end to build the pathway, the total height of the obstacle is the same: 600 feet below the finish line."

Michael, Marilyn and Amanda stepped behind the starting line. "Hey, Daddy, this mountain looks really high. Just how tall is it, do you think?"

"Oh, I would say as tall as the Tower of Food, if not taller. The M.I.A. is known to have some of the tallest structures ever created. Some have even reached out into space. The very top, of course, is made to protect us from the vacuum of space and the radiation of the sun. Our bodies can't handle that much electricity."
Amanda looked up again in a daze. "Oh, wow! That's tall!" She'd never felt dizziness before while looking up at a building, or on any ride, but this time she did, and she fainted.

Marilyn quickly leaned down and wrapped her daughter into her arms and fanned her with her free hand. "Amanda, wake up sweetie, are you okay?"

Michael looked on, worried. "Yes, Mom," Amanda muttered after regaining consciousness. "What happened? Why am I on the floor?"

Some of the workers at the M.I.A. rushed over and also question if she was okay, getting the same response she gave her mother. "Do you want to continue?" Asked one of the workers, in concern.

Michael and Marilyn looked at each other and then at Amanda. She replied, "Yes, of course! Are you kidding me? I'm fine everyone, I promise! I just got overwhelmed at the height of the mountain is all. I promise I'm able to do this."

"Okay, I'll take your word, little girl," replied a woman worker.

"I'm a woman, just like you," declared Amanda, trying to assert her independence and regain some dignity.

The woman looked at Marilyn and Michael and smiled. "I'm sorry, darling, my apologies. I'm sure a woman of your experience can handle this."

"I'm sure I can; I have been here before and have been in much higher situations."

The woman smiled again. "I'm sure you have. Now I wish you good luck in tonight's event, young woman, and to you both."

"Thank you," Amanda said politely, trying not to condescend toward the woman.

The voice over the loudspeakers buzzed through. "Will tonight's participants please report to the starting line for tonight's 7:30 event."

"Well, shall go we go, ladies?" Michael asked while holding out his arms to escort them.

"Yes, let's go, Daddy! Come on, Mom. I can't wait to see how we do. Do you think we'll win again?"

Marilyn looked at Amanda. "Maybe. I'm just happy we can be together like this. You're going to be quite busy next year with school, young lady. And remember, it's not about winning. As long as we get through it the right way, I'm happy."

A puzzled Amanda asked, "How could we do it the wrong way? Wouldn't that mean we lost if we did it the wrong way? I mean the object *is* to win, I thought. Doing it the wrong way would mean we came in last."

Marilyn smiled, "Awww, my precious, sure that's the object of this game. But I mean if we did things the wrong way, we would not work as a team and not listen to each other to try and solve the problems. Remember that's one of the reasons we have been winning all these; we play as a team and listen to each other's ideas. That's just how we live, darling. The same applies to this game. Understand?"

"Yes, Mommy, you're right. We do win most of the time playing that way. But we also lose, too. We've lost eight times to Gabriel, Angelina, and Max, and we've played against them 16 times. All those times we lost and we still tried as a team and listened to each other, and we still lost. Something doesn't add up to me."

"Sometimes both sides can be right and sometimes it's just about luck. Sometimes it's about who can execute a task faster or come up with a solution faster it's all just random, darling. Who knows, all those other teams we have played against and have beaten, maybe they only lose to us and there is a little girl or boy wondering the same thing you are right now. You never know."

"Wow, I never thought of that! Maybe there are families out there that only lose to us. Well, I still don't see the harm in trying something new every now and then. Maybe we will win against them next time we play them. But I'll listen to you and work as a team like we always do." Amanda reached up and hugged her mother.

Squeezing her tight, Marilyn said softly in her daughter's ear, "You're such a special being, Amanda, never forget that. You mean so much to me and you always will. I'm so happy that you can see both sides of the issues before making a decision. I know you'll always do the right thing." She kissed her forehead. "Now let's do this!"

The host stepped out of a doorway that just appeared in front of the starting line. Spotlights poured down on her and the crowd cheered for her presence. She raised her arm up above her golden blonde hair, with her forefinger in the air, thanking the audience and her fans, and then lowered her hand in a gesture for them to let her speak.

"Ladies and gentlemen and boys and girls from all over the universe, welcome!" The crowd cheered once again but even louder, then again it got quiet for her to continue. "Tonight's match is another classic between two families that have faced off many times before. Would you please welcome the blue team, consisting of Michael, his lovely wife, Marilyn, and their beautiful daughter, Amanda." As the wall slid away to reveal them, the crowd cheered again, and then awaited the introduction of their opponents. "Facing them again for the 17th time on the red team is Gabriel, his gorgeous wife, Angelina, and their handsome son, Maximilian." Again, the audience let out a boisterous cheer after they saw the red team. "Tonight they will compete in the 7:30pm maze created by last week's winners, Stephen, his wife JoAnne, and their son Jon." The spotlights then focus on a family standing just a couple of feet away and they wave, some more cheers are.

As the host talks to the winners of last week's maze, Michael walks Gabriel. "You sure know how to surprise me. I thought you were seeing Angelina's mother tonight."

"We will, buddy, later tonight. That's one of the best things about being a Modien, we don't get tired and our jobs are so short because we've been able to master the atom. Now, are you ready to get beat once again, my friend?"

Michael laughed at his best friend's insinuation that he will lose this time. "You don't know for sure that you will win, now do you buddy? We've played each other many times before and the outcome has been even so far. One thing is for sure about tonight: there will be a winner, but there will also be our friendship in the end."

"You got that right; you're like my brother and nothing will come between us. What do you think tonight's maze will be like? I've never built a bridge over a lava lake before, seems pretty interesting."

"I don't know, but you're right it—does sound interesting. Well, I'll see you on the other side?"

Gabriel grinned and put his hand out. Michael smiled and grasped his forearm, and their nano-bots blended together, forming one arm. This was something that not all Modiens could do; they have to have a special connection. No one was sure what exactly that connection was, because it varies from couple to couple, but Michael and Gabriel had had that special bond from childhood. "See you on the other side, my friend," Gabriel pulled back from his shoulder, and the long arm grew longer until it split back into the two arms of Michael and Gabriel.

The lights turned off and the whole arena went pitch black. The crowd yelled because they knew the games were about to begin. The announcer spoke again, "Contestants, on your marks, please; the race is about to begin." With that, the two families lined up at the bottom of the mountain specially made for tonight's maze.

The spotlights turned onto the host, her blue evening gown sparkled in the light from the rhinestones on her dress. She waved again before she said, "Remember, folks, tonight's audience is able to see the entirety of tonight's match through the special glass that surrounds the stands, which has been given to us by God to use just in this arena alone. They are able to see into the future and look at how the contestants are performing from the signals they emit from their Modien Essence Transmitters. Special receivers pick up those signals and translate them into a visual format, which is displayed across the glass. Now, who is ready for the fun to begin?" The crowd roared onto its feet and started chanting, "M.I.A.! M.I.A.!" They waited for the horns to blare the start of the race.

As soon as the horns sounded off to ignite the crowd, the two teams of friends started climbing the sides of the mountain designated for them. Amanda was fleet-footed; no one in her class could outrun her, and so far neither had Gabe, Angelina, or Max been able to match her speed. She quickly scaled the cliff and reached the plateau to push the first time warp button. Instantly, Michael and Marilyn were zapped thirty seconds into the future. They looked at the display screen to get the blueprints for the bridge and what materials it is made out of, and they scoured the area and started to build the bridge.

"Hey, that was easy," exclaimed Marilyn as she put the final piece of the bridge into place. The doorway opened and Amanda got zapped 30 seconds, plus the time it took for Michael and Marilyn to put the bridge together, into the future to meet up with them. "Hi, darling, was the other team almost done with their bridge?"

"Wow, that was quick! Good job, guys. Yeah, I think they are just about done moving their bridge into position with the crane, we'd better hurry. Gabriel and Angelina are fast builders, all right. I'm always amazed at how fast they can forge metals together. Oh well, let's look at how we can move this bridge." Amanda looked at the crane, the levitation device, length of the levers, and the length of the bridge, and estimated the length of the lava lake. "Well, I figure, if we use the levitation device twice, and four of the five levers, we would still only get across the bridge in more time than if we used the crane alone. Using the crane is the shortest amount of penalty we will get, but we don't know how fast it moves. However, I think, if we use the levitation device three times, that will bring the bridge just over two thirds of the way over the lake, then we can just use the levers to pole vault the rest of the way and save us a good 20 seconds at the least."

"Awww, sweetie, that's awfully dangerous; there's no net above the lava and the bridge will only be a few feet above the lake as it is. I don't think that's a good idea. We can make it up in the last stage."

Frustrated, Amanda started using the levitation device to move the bridge and said, "There's no time to make it up on the other end." She pointed to the scoreboard, which indicated the other team was almost on the other side of the lake using the crane. "Look since they built the bridge faster they can afford to use the crane!

"Besides, the levers are long enough for us to reach the other side. Watch." Amanda grabbed a lever and started running to the end of the bridge. She placed one end of the lever down in front of her and lifted herself up and over the rest of the lake with ease. She landed on her feet and turned around, yelling, "See how easy that was? Now it's your turn!"

Michael and Marilyn looked at each other and smiled, and they both picked up a lever and hurled themselves across the fiery lake to land next to Amanda. Michael shouted, "That was brilliant, sweetheart. Now push the time-warp button."

Marilyn shot her daughter a look for disobeying her, but she said nothing.

Amanda smiled not seeing her mother's face, and smacked down the button. Instantly, they are thrust into the future two minutes, and they saw the location of the starting point for the final stage of the maze. They spread out to find the particular spot on the mountain.

"Here it is!" shouted Amanda. "I've found it! Come on, hurry! We have to push the button!" Michael and Marilyn ran to her and she pushed the button. "Almost done!" he exclaimed excitedly, and they were all sent backward one minute and 59 seconds into the past.

Marilyn found a computer screen next to the building point and read out the numbers "Two, eight, 17, and then the missing number, then 44 and the last number, 62."

Michael quickly answered, "Twenty-nine!"

"Are you sure? If I enter the wrong number in, the wrong size pieces will be made, we could wind up hundreds of feet short."

"Yes, I'm positive. The increase of the numbers in the sequence is three. It goes from two to eight and then from eight to 17, an increase from six to nine. Then, if 29 works, the increase from 17 to 29 is 12, then it would be 15 more to 44, and 18 more to 62."

Marilyn smiled and input the number 29 into the computer, and 29 pieces, just over 10 feet each, materialized. "I think we got it; here's the next sequence: Three hundred eight, and then the missing number, 541, 674, 818."

This time Amanda answered, "The missing number is 419."

"That's what I think, too. How about you, Michael?"

"Yup, sounds about right to me. Go for it, darling."

Marilyn entered 419 into the computer and out came 419 pieces just over eight inches each. "Wow, that's a lot of pieces," Marilyn exclaimed. "I hope this works." She pushed the button to assemble all 448 pieces to create a pathway, which materialized out of the huge wall next to them. They positioned it to the top of the mountain and climbed it to the finish line to win.

After the celebrations of victory and the interview with the host, Michael walked over to Gabriel. "Hey, man, I saw on the replay that you guys were just a few hundredths of a second behind us finishing. I didn't realize it was that close."

"I know, I think that was one of our closest matches ever. I thought we had you crossing the lake, but you guys took a risk and wound up beating us. Congratulations, my friends! That was fun!" Gabriel hugged Marilyn and gave her a kiss on the cheek, and did the same to Amanda. "I just hope I get to play in the maze you guys come up with for next week. I can't believe all these times you all have won that we've never played the maze you get to make."

"I don't get that, either. Maybe I can arrange something for next week—well, not me, Marilyn."

Angelina looked over at Marilyn. "How can you arrange something like that? No one other than diplomats can request who participates in the maze they make."

Smiling, Marilyn answered, "Well, nothing is official, but I have been offered a job as a diplomat. I had to ask these two if it was okay if I went before I could tell the High Coalition of Space-Traveling Beings that I accept."

"Wow, that's incredible Marilyn! How come you didn't tell me sooner?"

"I was waiting for the dinner party to tell you guys; I didn't expect to see you here tonight."

Angelina grinned at her friend. "I'm terribly happy for you—I know you've wanted to be a diplomat since childhood. Do you know yet where you're to be stationed?"

Marilyn, of course, couldn't reveal that kind of sensitive information yet, not until it was official that she was a diplomat. "I don't know yet; it could be anywhere. I could be gone for a long time … months … maybe even a year."

"Wow! Can you come back for holidays or a vacation?"

"No, the travel time is too long, although I hear our kind is going to be able to travel faster than light soon. I guess the initial ban on our species is under review and a lift is being considered. Can you imagine that? Traveling back in time, seeing how actual members of the Old lived, even those things called dinosaurs!"

"It's going to be a wonderful time for our species indeed. So, I suppose that means our species must not be much of a threat to the High Coalition of Space-Traveling Beings, and hopefully then you can come back home at will. I'm going to miss you."

"I'm going to miss you, too, but enough of this sappy stuff. Let's go eat; I'm starving. Winning makes me so hungry," Marilyn laughed in a teasing manner.

The two families waved to the crowd for a final time and headed off to the restaurant to eat dinner, relax from the night's event and talk about it, and talk about their lives, much like they usually do after playing inside the Maze of Inter-Dimensional Aliment.

Once they were finished eating, Gabriel stood up from the table. "Well, this has been a delight. I can't wait to do it again, but we must get going now. Angelina's mother is waiting for us. I think we're supposed to see Titan, actually. I heard Marilyn did a great job with terraforming it into another living place for us."

Marilyn stood up, followed quickly by Michael. "Thanks Gabe, I hope I did. Crystal is supposed to finish up; she deserves it, and she's been working so hard lately and seems so lonely. I'm hoping to fix her up with a co-worker."

Michael laughed in his head at his wife playing match-maker. "Yes, she thinks those two will have a great future together. Actually I can see that happening; they do have a great rapport."

Angelina politely said, "Well I know it'll be terrific, just like the others you've worked on."

"Thanks, Ange, that means a lot to me. I've been so lucky with my terraforming, but that chapter of my life is over now. It's time to be a diplomat. My dream is finally coming true! I've accomplished all that I wanted to. Well, so far."

"Cheers!" Gabriel shouted out in excitement, and they all raised their glasses to Marilyn.

Having said their goodbyes, they headed out to their cars, Michael reminding them that they had dinner plans later that week.

A couple of days later, Gabriel, Angelina and Max went to Michael and Marilyn's; they were to have a couple of drinks before they all headed off to Jacob's for dinner. They knocked on the door and Amanda answered, "Hi! Mom and Dad aren't ready yet, they should be out soon. Where are the twins?" Angelina laughed lightly and replied that they were sleeping in the back of the car, and to be very quiet. Amanda ran over to look in the window of the car and said, "They look like babies, and they're supposed to be twins? How come one has more hair than the other?"

Gabe and Angelina both started laughing. "Oh, my dear," said Angelina, "that's just how they're growing up. They both were bald when they were first made, but one started growing hair, then the other just started yesterday."

"Wow, so they're really different, then? I thought twins acted the same and looked the same. I never expected this," she giggled. "They're soooo cute."

"Why, thank you, Amanda." Gabriel picked them up and brought them inside to the family room of the house. The hairier twin woke up and started crying. Within seconds, the other woke up and cried, too. "Have you ever fed a baby?"

"No, just my dolls," replied Amanda, pointing over to her life-like doll that was sucking its thumb.

Gabriel looked at Angelina for approval, and she nodded. "Here." He handed Elizabeth, whom they'd decided to call Lizbeth, to Amanda. "Cradle her and gently place the bottle over her lips; she knows what to do from then on."

Amanda did as she was told and saw that the infant guzzled down the milk, smiling and humming. She looked up at Gabe and Angelina, smiling proudly and enjoying her first time feeding a little baby. "I don't think it's fair I have to wait over ANOTHER 191 years to have one of my own." Gabriel and Angelina looked at each and smirked. "Why do babies sleep and I don't? I thought we never slept because we don't need to."

"Infants need sleep because their circuitry is still connecting to form the final stages of growth. All of us sleep for only a year. Then, all the neurons that connect to our Vial of Viability are completed through teeny-tiny openings," explained Angelina.

"Wow, so I *slept?* I had no idea! Why wasn't I told this before?"

"You will find out everything you need to know next year in school when you get your Big Bang. Look, Alexa wants to be fed, too." She took Lizbeth from Amanda and handed her the other twin. They both smiled as Alexa started to guzzle the milk in the same manner as her sister, humming and smiling. Miraculously, right then, some more hair started to sprout on her head, just enough to match her sister's growth. "Would you look at that! That almost never happens to an infant when it's not one of the parents feeding it. You must be someone special, Amanda!"

Marilyn, who had just emerged from the dressing area, looked over at the two. "That's incredible, sweetheart! I always knew you were mommy's little angel. I have such a strong feeling you are going to be some one important!"

A puzzled Amanda just shrugged. "It's just fun! Look how cute they are! They love their milk. Alexa's hungry; she hasn't stopped yet."

Out came Michael and, seeing his daughter acting so mature and caring for the newborn, thought that this is as good as it gets, his loving family and friends all together. Later they'd all go to spend a wonderful evening with his grandfather. He sighed in content.

Seconds later, he was thinking about how things might have been for the earlier race. The ones that were alive before the Switch, when living was tough and sickness was rampant. He thought of Jacob being sick, and what might become of him … and another burst of light blinded Michael. He prepared himself for whatever his father might have in store for him when he woke up in a dream that felt so real it brought nothing but fear.

After waking up and seeing his surroundings, once again Michael realized he'd had another black out, and remembered the conversation with his father about how God wasn't who he said he was, and his accusation that he had hate inside him. Michael closed his eyes and turned away, his head lowered. "You don't know me at all, Dad. You never have. You were too busy with everything else and everyone else. You wanted to be like God, even after you heard those things all those years ago. You wanted all his attention and to show to him that *you* are the perfect being He always envisioned once He set out to create us Modiens. You're the one full of hate, not me."

"And that's something new, my child? Yes, I am full of hate, that's something we already know. Yet I only found out about this hatred recently—surprising, isn't it? For centuries after I lost my wife and soon-to-be son, I felt something inside me that I wasn't quite sure of, something I could never put my finger on. It left me feeling empty, though, I know that. And this void grew day by day, year after year, century after agonizing century. Then, shortly before you were born, I decided to try again to have a child. Only I couldn't bear the pain of finding a love and to potentially lose her again." A tear swelled in Daniel's eye, but he fought it back and continued, "Once I had you, I was full of joy and excitement once again. For the first few years of your life, I was a new person. You were everything, my world. I wanted you to be the perfect child of the perfect race. Something I didn't get the chance for with Jeremiah."

Michael sat there listening to his father, wondering what changed. Where did all that affection and attention go and why? The only thing he could remember while growing up was that his father was always showing off his son. How proud he was of him. He smiled at such memories. Then he remembered that around the age of five, things started to change between them. His father grew more and more distant, for what only seemed to prove to God his worthiness. At first, he stopped talking to him as much, and then he stopped showing as much affection. At the time, Michael figured this was how things went when growing up, and that this was normal. Then more memories flooded his vision of the other kids, friends of his, and how their parents never stopped showing that affection, even to this day.

"Michael, what are you doing? I am asking you something; I would appreciate your attention," Daniel barked at Michael. "Now, as I was saying. It took me a very long time to figure out that A.T.M.s and the Machine of Forever could do certain things, but I have."

"You have what? I stopped listening, I think; I went into a day dream."

"You're kidding, right?"

"No, I'm sorry! I was just wondering what it was like for God to be only part of the creation of a new species. I mean, even us Modiens have complete control over *our* Homo sapiens in our universes. How come God wasn't given complete control over them?" He left out the other thoughts of the memories of his childhood, thinking that by divulging that information to his father would only make him angrier, and would result in yet another slap and jolting in this "electric chair."

"That's a good question, my boy. I asked him that once. He confessed how He wasn't the *only* supreme being that created mankind, but one of many."

"What'd he say?"

"He told me that as long as He was being honest, He might as well tell the whole truth. Although, I still have a feeling He was holding some things back. He said He was chosen to be part of this group to create the Homo sapiens, and that He is more like us, Modified-Sapiens, than the Homo sapiens. He said that He was part of an experiment to create a new species and to help them evolve. He said the reason so many were chosen was to better understand how beings dealt with compromising and getting along with others. That creating a new race demanded such skills, and the fact that He was one of the best that could understand the plight of others and see their point of view, He was chosen as one of the leaders of that group." Daniel stopped talking, remembering how he felt when he heard how He said He had to make tough decisions about what knowledge was allowed to be given to the Homo sapiens and what was to be kept from them until a later time. "Now, all of this was shocking, to say the least, as you can imagine. He then asked me how I felt about hearing his confession."

"Well, what did you say?"

"What was I going to say, Michael? Was I going to tell Him off and call him a fraud to His face? What did I know, then? Back then I was His friend, I was someone He trusted and someone He cared about. I was given life by Him, a life much better than His previous creation, and I knew it and was grateful. I … loved Him, and He loved me." Daniel paused as a tear rolled off his sharp jaw.

"Dad … what did you say?"

"I told Him not to worry about it, that He was the same person He was before He confessed. I even told Him how proud I was for that and that I would be there for Him, forever."

"What changed?"

Another tear ran down Daniel's face. "Death happened, a death that should never have happened, not then, not ever." He stood up, wiped his cheek, pounded his fist on the table and declared, "But, I will have my Jessica back one day soon, and with my new wife, Manaba, I will finally have that spark in that person I've tried to clone many times before but couldn't.

With Amanda's help, though, I will have my wife, my love, my Jessica, back. Amanda's vision of her grandmother is just how I remember her, the same wit and sense of humor, the same timing of her jokes, she even smells the same. With Amanda's help, I'll clone Manaba and only Amanda with her knowledge of female genes can add the traits and qualities I couldn't conceive of being a man. Once my new wife and I leave here with your daughter, I will have my revenge on 'God' and 'He' will fail greater than anyone has failed before. You hear me now, Michael? Your precious 'God' will have a failure even greater than Satan himself had, and there's nothing you can do about it, being trapped in here."

"There's something I don't get, though, Father. If God isn't who He says He is, then who is? And who is Satan if he exists beyond being caged here on New Earth?"

Daniel sat back down for a second, then sipped from his glass of wine once again. "I don't know who the *real* God is, my son. I believe that *is* the real Satan caged up, though, and I do believe the Mysorians support him to the fullest, and there's nothing wrong with having some muscle on your side. They are an advanced species, maybe even more than us, if that's possible. I mean, they have the ability to shape shift, they can blend in with any species with ease, virtually undetectable. They have vast knowledge of the universe, again maybe more than us. And, best of all, they, for whatever reason, have a very strong grudge against God and seem to like me and my ideas very much and wish me to succeed. They're planning on supporting me until the end."

Michael interrupted, "The end? The end of what?"

Daniel once again pounded his fist on the table. "If you'd let me finish you'd know by now, now wouldn't you, son?" He waited for a decisive answer from his son.

"Yes, Father, please. I'm starting to understand more where you are coming from. I had no idea things were the way were for you; I can sort of understand why you're so mad. I wouldn't want to lose Marilyn, I know that."

Daniel looked down at his son as he stood up. "There will never be another time like this, my son. Wake up and see what is to come, what Amanda and I will bring to the Modien race. You can either be with us, or against us. Either way, it will happen. I will usher in a new age of wisdom. There will be a new age of knowledge and power, but, more importantly, a new age of learning, through evil, and I will be on top. I'll achieve what Satan couldn't!"

"You're insane! Modiens are too smart to allow anything like that to happen again! Modiens know the consequences of having evil in society; we've learned from our previous form, the Homo sapiens, the Old. Our bodies are even designed to block as much as that side as possible."

"You're STILL disappointing me, Michael. Don't you understand? They don't know anything about what I'm offering. They will clamor, claw, and yes, even murder, to know what I know. It's just in our nature to learn new things. We are beings of pure consciousness. We're capable of storing countless bytes of information, and are able to use that information at a moment's notice. We THRIVE on new information. We CRAVE it! I saw it each time I came back from diplomatic missions, from the very first expeditions outside of our solar system to other civilizations in other galaxies. The people couldn't get that information fast enough. I saw it with my own eyes, Michael. Now you will see it. That is, if you decide to join us. I'm giving you one last chance, Michael. Yes or no?"

"Never! There will be an end to this evil! God wouldn't let Satan escape on the New Earth and spread his evil ways on humankind again. He made sure of that when He entrapped him inside the Cage of Satan. Since then, Satan hasn't been able to influence mankind. Not the Old, and not even us, Father. Satan's time on the New Earth is over. God wouldn't have left otherwise. Modiens know enough not to look at the Pother for too long. We know the risks. We're smart enough not to threaten our way of life."

"Our way of life has been stifled since day one! I am the very example of what was to be 'God's' perfect creation, but He was wrong about us, just like the Mysorians. And when 'God' left to fight Satan elsewhere, my boy, He didn't count on his perfect creation to realize that there is much more to life than what was given. He didn't count on one of His own creations to defy the death that was handed to him as part of the cards of life, even though it was without his consent to pass on to begin with, and since *I* defied death, my son, it goes against God's wishes. But no one wants to die, or pass on, or whatever fancy words you want to call it; that's why God himself is immortal. You know that and I know that.

"The Mysorians have always supported me; they were the only other species that agreed with me that Modiens should never die, at least not me, the very first Modified-Sapiens. I heard when they found out I passed on, they were quite disappointed, since they wanted to see more ideas from me. That's why I'm going to arrange for them to come to the New Earth for a truce between our kinds. And they'll see how God is gone and His powers won't harm them anymore while they are on the New Earth. Then they will see Satan is still caged and see how he is still useless to them. With the rest of the Coalition not showing up for the meeting, for reasons unknown, the Mysorians will be very mad indeed. They will demand an answer just as you are now. I'll make them wait until they are just about ready to leave. Then I'll calm them down when I walk into the room and reassure them that a truce is indeed most acceptable.

"I'll tell them what I told you, how this being isn't *the God* but just another being of high intelligence like every other in the universe. I'll tell them how I escaped my cage when Satan couldn't escape his. The Mysorians will love it and want more from me, just like they did when I was alive. Excuse me—alive the *first* time. I brought myself back from death, after all; I forget that too, sometimes."

"So, you know what the Mysorians want now? Don't make me laugh, Father."

"Go ahead and laugh away. Would I lie to you?"

"Lie to me? It seems you've been telling me lies my whole life! What else don't I know? Tell me! I demand to know!" Michael struggled too much once again and the shocks coursed through his body, rendering him motionless for a few seconds. He then woke up to seeing Amanda holding one of the twins and Marilyn talking to him. He shook his head and remembered where he was, at his house, about to go to Jacob's for dinner. He still knew that the dream would continue once again. He just didn't know when.

"Oh, Michael, guess what just happened with our daughter?"

"I think she's done," announced Amanda to Angelina. "Now what?"

"Here, I'll take her." Angelina lifted Alexa out of Amanda's arms and wiped her mouth. She placed the baby over her shoulder and started patting her back lightly. Alexa burped and giggled. "Awww, that's my little angel."

"No idea. What'd I miss?" Asked Michael, smiling at Alexa's burping, trying to forget that horrible scene.

"Tell Daddy, Amanda," said Marilyn.

"Well, I don't know what all the fuss is about. I was just feeding the twins, the one with less hair grew more hair, and that's all I got from it. And now everyone thinks I'm this super special person or something." Michael looked over at the glint in Marilyn's eyes and smiled. "What's it mean, Daddy?"

He walked over to Amanda, cupped her cheeks and kissed her forehead. "It means you are indeed someone special that is going to play an important role in the world one day. It's not every day an infant grows hair while being fed by someone *other than her parents*. This means, one day you could be a diplomat to another planet, or an incredible inventor of something no one has ever thought of before. The universe has no limit for you. You're going to make a huge impact in life one day." He gave her another kiss on the forehead, and the whole room grew into a comfortable calmness and unity; they realized the significance of the situation.

Amanda just stood there, smiling, starting to understand just how important she was, and felt this energy, this new extraordinary emotion coursing through her entire body, and it felt better than accomplishment or the feeling of doing a job well. She didn't know it was her ego, but it delighted her to no end; she'd never felt such energy could exist, and she wanted more.

Suddenly a bolt of lightning jolted across the sky, waking the twins into hysterical fits. Gabriel quickly picked up the scared Lizbeth and tried to calm her down as Angelina did the same with Alexa. It took a couple of minutes for them to finally relax enough to stop crying from the lightning, but they were having trouble falling asleep.

"Let's try riding in the car to get them back to sleep," suggested Gabriel. She agreed, and they gathered their belongings for the trip to Jacob's.

"Sounds like a good idea; it is over a half hour away," said Michael. "I know Jacob is excited about seeing everyone again, and I don't want to keep him waiting. Is everyone ready?"

"Just a second, darling. I have to change my outfit; this one doesn't feel right for the occasion." Marilyn walked to the dressing room and into the H.A.T.M.L.; her outfit instantly changed to something to better suit her mood. "Ah, this feels better," she told everyone as she came out again. "Let's go see Jacob, now, shall we?"

The two families got into their cars and headed off to Jacob's house. Michael, Gabe and the twins took the newly made mini-van-looking vehicle that Angelina had designed for the twins, while Marilyn, Angelina and Amanda rode in Michael's 1967 GTO Sport Coupe.

"Wow, this car sure looks old," Angelina remarked in a joking manner.

"I think it's unique, just like Michael," said Marilyn. "The car, his taste for s'mores, and his love for classical music make me look at things differently. Sort of appreciate Jacob and his kind more. They never had things as easy as we do now, and I think Michael realizes that, and that's why he isn't more in the public eye. I always get asked why he isn't out in the spotlight more, you know, being a grandson of the Old and the son of the first Modified-Sapiens."

Angelina smiled, "That's just not Michael, though. Even I know that."

"Yeah, he's very modest. I asked him once just after we had met. He barely talked back then about why he didn't he have a more high profile job like a diplomat, and he said he wouldn't get to use his mind as much. Then I asked why he hardly ever talked."

"And?"

"He told me, 'It's because no one ever talked to him.' I thought how that was a really interesting answer, so I started talking to him more. He is just … so incredibly caring once you get to know him, and very smart. He's someone special, not just to me and Amanda, and I can tell he will do something great someday, just as we saw with Amanda tonight. I feel very lucky indeed."

Angelina nodded, "I see it, too, and I noticed that with Gabe. Maybe we're just love struck." They both chuckled some, enjoying the scenery changing from the tall skyscrapers to a thick, lush forest.

In the other car, Michael and Gabriel talked about what Michael had heard from his father and grandfather. "So," Gabriel asked, "what do you think is going on? What'd your father say about colds and viruses?"

"I didn't get much; he didn't even seem himself last time. I can't quite put my finger on it, but something was different. I didn't like it."

"How so?" questioned Gabriel as he handed Michael a cappuccino.

"He just seemed to have this attitude like he was better than me. I don't ever remember him acting like that before, or anyone acting like that before."

"Wow," exclaimed Gabe. "I don't know what to say. I've always remembered him as humble as you, if not more so. I mean, sure, he occasionally enjoyed being out in front, but he was our first. He was thrust upon the scene in the universe and shined as bright as the spotlight cast on him."

"I know; maybe it's nothing. Maybe he is just happy that he found someone that looks like my mom. He's even marrying her."

"Really? I had no idea that could happen, but I guess that's just his version of heaven."

"Yeah, he did seem really happy he found someone that looks just like Jessica. It was eerie, the similarity, actually; I've only seen pictures and holograms of her. He must have been looking all these years for someone that looks like her."

"Well, at least he's happy, right, buddy?"

"True. I remember him saying once how much he missed Jessica. I wish I had known her, she seemed like an amazing woman."

"Yes, it's a shame they couldn't get her to the Ball of Essence for Daniel to be with her once he had passed on."

"Yeah, I wouldn't know what I would do if I couldn't see Marilyn again after I pass on."

"Me, too. Gabriel added, as he finished his cappuccino, "My world is Angelina and my children."

Just then, the two vehicles arrived at Jacob's house. Michael knocked on the front door, and they all waited for the old man to answer. "I don't have a good feeling," Angelina said reluctantly after about 30 seconds. "Something is not right." Michael knocked on the door again; still there was no answer. He placed his hand into the security scanner, the door opened, and they saw Jacob on the floor, coughing uncontrollably.

"Grandpa!" Michael rushed over to him. "Quick, get him some water!" He picked Jacob up and brought him over to the couch. "It's okay; we're here now, Grandpa. Someone call Doctor Kimberly!"

Marilyn went to the monitor and requested emergency medical care; within seconds Doctor Kimberly appeared from the H.A.T.M.L. and started scanning Jacobs's body. "How long has he been like this?"

"We don't know, we just arrived and he was like this. Please help him!" pleaded Marilyn.

A syringe of antibiotics and other medications materialized, and Doctor Kimberly injected Jacob with the needle. He stopped coughing immediately and sat up on the couch, wiping his mouth. He took a deep breath.

"Michael. I'm sorry, Michael. I am dying."

Michael, still holding his grandfather, replied, "No, you're going to be fine, Grandpa. We will get through this. We'll figure out a way to get you better. I promise."

"No, Michael. I'm afraid there's nothing more that can be done for me; it's just a matter of time before I pass on."

Amanda started crying and shouted, "You can't die, Great Grandpa! You just can't! It's not fair!"

"Awww, my poor child, come here." Jacob motioned for her to sit next to him. "No more tears, my dear child." He wiped them away and tried to reassure her that he would still be around. "You just have to visit me inside the Machine of Forever."

"But why do you have to be confined to that one spot? How come when we pass on we can only stay inside the Building of Souls? Why can't we just live forever on the New Earth?"

"Awww, darling, it was just our deal with God. Besides, I'm told you don't feel like you're trapped inside it. It'll be just like heaven, and I'm sure heaven isn't confined, right?"

"I suppose, it's just I'm going to miss you." She wrapped her arms around his body and hugged him, giving him a kiss on the cheek. Once again, Jacob started coughing, causing Amanda to run behind her father for protection from the unknown.

"I'm sorry, everyone. I wanted to have a pleasant dinner. I guess the cold is getting worse."

"Speaking of which, Jacob, what do you think is causing this cold and all these Modiens to get infected with "viruses?" asked Gabriel. "Is there anything I can get for you now?"

"I have no idea what's causing all this sickness. Could you bring the FFF over so I can get a cup of tea, please, Gabe?" Gabe found the FFF and pulled it over to Jacob on the couch. He pulled out a soothing cup of tea with some honey. He blew the steam away and sipped the tea. "I have a feeling something bad is coming."

"Bad? Like what, Grandpa?"

"I don't know, but I have had this feeling deep within me, one that I haven't felt since before the Switch."

"What do you think it is, though, Jacob?" asked Angelina. "What feeling would you get before the Switch?"

"I can't put my finger on it, but it feels like trouble is coming." He started coughing uncontrollably again and spit up some blood this time. Everyone was shocked into silence and had no idea how to react to such a thing. No one got sick in the Modien world, not even when a member of the Old passed away. They didn't die from any sickness; they just passed away in their sleep. "Please, everyone, I'll be fine; don't look so worried. Amanda, come here, my darling child." He extended his hand out and caressed her cheek. "Remember how much I love you, and always remember that you have something special in you. You will do something extraordinarily important. I don't know what, but I can feel it in you." He gave her a kiss on the forehead. Looking back with tears in her eyes, Amanda was puzzled, not knowing what to say, so she just hugged him and cried. "Hey, hey, no more crying. Please, all of you, I'll be okay; you can always see me in the Machine of Forever. Don't feel sad. Now is the time you have to be strong, stick together and—"

"But Jacob," interrupted Angelina, "why do you say such things? What is it you feel that's coming? How do you know it is bad?"

"I don't know, I just have always had bad feelings right before a bad event would occur; it's been that way for as long as I can remember. They usually come true, too."

"Like what?" asked Gabriel.

"Oh, I don't know. I had one of the worst feelings I've ever had right before the Apocalypse. Or like how right before Wormwood hit, this feeling came over me to go to the basement and look for something...." He stopped, realizing for the first time his mortality. "I had no idea what it was I should be looking for when I got down there, but it didn't matter. I woke up later with everything gone. My family and friends all destroyed, in what I'm told was just seconds of pure hell raining down. Being so close to the impact, many wondered, including myself, how I survived at all. Anyway, I have always had these premonitions, and I haven't had one since before the Switch. I don't know if I just don't remember the feelings, or if this one is just particularly bad in nature. Whatever it is, it's bad. I'm not sure what will come of it, but this bad event feels very close, like it's going to involve one of us. Try to stick together and remember the love you have for each other." He started coughing again as everyone looked at each other; just then the vehicle arrived that would take Jacob away to a place the Old called a hospital. Doctor Kimberly, Michael and Marilyn all rode with Jacob, praying he'd get better again.

Part II

The Solution Is Near?

Life went on for almost a year, and Jacob's health deteriorated even with all the advancements in nano-technology. The cause of this cold of Jacob's had eluded detection, and every medicine tried had failed to make him feel better for any significant amount of time.

Amanda was about to reach her Big Bang and get her very own Starter Atomic Transference Machine once she turned 10. She had excelled in her studies and learned at a phenomenal rate. She'd even started protesting to have her own S.A.T.M. 10 months earlier, much to the dismay of having to be told over and over again she had to wait until she turned 10 and to be patient because it was only a little bit away.

Michael was coping with the fact he was going to lose his grandfather at any moment. He often visited Jacob, who was switching stays between his place and the hospital. He was thankful that the horrid visions he had of himself being held hostage to his father had stopped after that night they first found Jacob sick at his house. Life was pretty good still, even with Jacob being sick. Every so often, Michael even visited Daniel, only to be rushed through, Daniel stating he was far too busy with this new project that he was working on, and Michael thought how nothing had changed with him, after all. He was the same father he always remembered and that one brief moment after he met that woman that resembled his mother had been a fluke. All that attention he paid Michael was just a show for her, trying to impress her before they got married.

Marilyn, as usual, was there, at least remotely, to support him and cheer him up. She was also trying to finish a deal with a species for a trade, one that would ensure safety between the two and a trade route for various goods and services. She'd left five months before to travel to the planet she was trying to solidify the deal with and she would be gone for one more month.

Gabriel and Angelina were busy with the twins; luckily Max was helping as much as he could, and even Amanda went over sometimes and helped. The twins were growing up fast, already walking and talking. Gabriel and Angelina were finding out that the twins did share some thoughts and feelings, just as Angelina's grandmother and her sister had. Angelina had been inventing some extraordinary pieces of music recently and had been asked to create an opera for the same planet Marilyn was working with, so she'd gone with Marilyn. Gabriel and Michael were spending more time together, almost as much time as when they'd grown up together. They were both having a blast raising their children, yet missed their wives and couldn't wait for their return next month, just in time for Amanda's Big Bang.

After work one day, Michael came home to an empty house. No Amanda, no Brody, no noise.
He figured Amanda had taken Brody for a walk, and he decided to wait. But after half an hour and no sign of his daughter, Michael started to get a bad feeling and went out looking for her. Knowing how she wanted to have her own Starter Atomic Transference Machine more than just about anything else in the world, Michael decided to look at the T.A.T.M.S., but with no luck.

He checked the Building of Souls to visit Daniel and ask him if he had seen Amanda. Upon arrival, he looked inside and saw a dense jungle that had somehow grown in the entrance, and that the Sentinel of Souls was gone, and there were no visitors. Somehow, he knew his daughter was here; a sense of dread grew in the pit of his stomach. He walked farther inside the jungle and shouted, "Father. Father! Show yourself! Where is she? Where's Amanda?"

"Father...." Amanda walked out from behind a tree.

"Amanda! Are you okay, angel?"

"Oh, Daddy! You always ask such silly questions," she giggled in response.

"Come down here, darling. Let's go home. We're already in trouble. You had me worried, you've been gone for so long."

"But why, Daddy? I'm having fun like how you told me to do, don't you remember?"

Michael was stunned at what he'd just heard from his precious little girl. The thought of her thinking of breaking the rules as "fun" overwhelmed him; minors going inside the Machine of Forever without a parent was strictly forbidden. He shouted for Daniel again. "Show yourself, Father. What have you done to her? You know she's not allowed in here without me!"

"Oh, Daddy, you have no idea what you're up against, here. I've learned so much; I can do so much. Much more than anyone can ever imagine. And, what Grandpa Daniel has planned for me, it's all just about to start, Daddy. You're going to be so proud of me, Daddy; just wait and see what I've learned in my first time ever inside an A.T.M.... Well, second."

"Amanda! You stop this now! You're better than this. You can do so much good—why are you doing this? Don't you know how much trouble we're already in?" Michael tried to climb up a fallen tree to get to the small cliff where Amanda was standing, but the tree crumbled beneath his feet halfway up and he fell to back to the ground.

"I'm not stopping anything, Daddy. They have to learn." She started swinging on a vine that was hanging off the tree next to her.

"Learn? Learn what, baby? What can be learned from doing all that to the lobby of the Building of Souls? You know you can't be in here without me. And I don't know what you did to the Sentinel of Souls and all the visitors, but you have to stop this now!"

"Oh, Father, you will find out … you *all* will find out." She stopped swinging, raised her arm up and opened her fist, palm facing up. Hundreds of her nano-bots flew out of it, and started racing toward Michael. He screamed while trying to cover up. The creatures tore at him, ripping pieces of flesh off him, and trails of sparks flew off from the gaping holes left behind. His nano-bots quickly tried to repair the damage, but without the raw materials they get from his food, the best they could do for Michael was break off the damaged pieces, making him that much smaller, with fewer nano-bots.

"Amanda, why?" Michael looked down at his wounds; he'd never seen such a thing before in his life. The remaining nano-bots quickly repaired the rest of his wounds so no further damage could occur, but something was wrong. He'd lost some memory, he could tell. He tried to remember how he met Marilyn and couldn't. He even forgot the love he felt from her and all the memories he had of them together. He'd lost the look on her face when she said yes when he'd asked if she'd marry him; he even had forgotten the birth of Amanda. All he could remember of Marilyn now was just that they were married and had a daughter together.

"Why, Daddy, you always told me to try to learn something new each day, and you're always telling me that I am someone special. I'm just trying to live up to the potential you see in me." She motioned for her nano-bots to strike her father again. They scraped off thousands more nano-bots, creating more sparks to fly out of the gashes. Michael lost all memory of his childhood and all the basic knowledge that Modiens acquire by the age of ten. To Modified-Sapiens, that period of learning is quite essential to being highly functional. Amanda's attack had actually made her father's I.Q. as low as a Homo sapiens.

Losing that many nano-bots at once had also disrupted the balance of electricity a Modien needs to keep his nano-bots reading his Modien Essence Transmitter. Michael fell over to the ground. "Amanda...." He looked up at her smiling down as she slowly walked toward him. "Amanda, I love you ... why?

"Never mind that now, Michael," Daniel shouted out from atop the small waterfall breaking out of the thick jungle that had grown inside the Building of Souls; the water started flowing faster down past Michael and out the door. "Let's go inside, my boy, and then you will see why." Daniel picked his son up and carried him off into the depths of the jungle.

Slung over his fathers' shoulder, Michael saw the tribe's people he'd seen earlier when he was taken to meet Daniel's new wife. He only has the strength to say, "Amanda..." before he passed out.

Michael woke up feeling extremely weak and disillusioned. He didn't remember where he was or how he got there. He looked around and saw Amanda sitting on the stone floor, playing with something he couldn't quite make out. He smiled at the sight of her, forgetting the things she had done to him. Perhaps he just didn't want to believe his child could do such things; perhaps it was easier to deny what happened. That was a lie, though. He remembered, but he had to push that thought aside now and figure out how to deal with his situation. "Where am I? Is this a dream I'm having again?"

"No, my son; this is really happening to you; this is no dream. I know you remember what happened, so quit playing dumb."

"Father, you have to stop this NOW. It is still your choice to end this. Tell Amanda to stop, I beg of you!"

"Oh, my boy, this is only the beginning. I have great plans for the future, and Amanda is going to be the key to it all. She's going to bring in a new era of life, a new form of living that has been absent since the beginning of the Modien existence."

Baffled, Michael tried to stand up but fell back into the chair behind him, still very weak from electrical flux he suffered. "You leave Amanda out of this, do you hear me? How could you do this? Why? Why do you need her?" He struggled to free himself but couldn't—even though his anger was giving him some strength, it wasn't nearly enough.

"I've told you, but if you want a more detailed explanation, I shall enlighten you." Daniel walked over to sit beside Michael. He lifted his only son's face with his index finger. "Chin up, my son," he said mockingly. "She will be fine, I promise, which is more than I can say for my first child."

Again Michael is taken aback. "Your *what*?"

"Don't be naïve! I was 650 when I had you; there had been three generations that came before you, and yet *I* was the *first* Modien. Ever wonder why I was so old when you were born?"

Michael thought back to his childhood. Most of it was gone, but he remembered hearing some people say how proud they were of Daniel for having Michael after all those years and never understanding why they would say such a thing. He figured his father had waited that long to have him because he was busy, nothing more.

Then he remembered hearing his father give a speech at a ceremony between Modiens and the first civilization discovered outside the Milky Way Galaxy, saying that he felt alone and empty after his loss, but after all this time, finally, this burgeoning relationship with the new intergalactic race made him feel somewhat whole again. That he vowed to spend the rest of his life trying to not only strengthen this new relationship, but to create other diplomatic relationships with other peaceful beings across the universe, uniting them all as one.

Michael had never understood at the time what that "loss" had referred to; he'd only been five at the time and far too excited about the new technologies that were just starting to be shared with the Modiens. "I remember you saying how the new establishments made you feel whole again … you had had a child before me? How come you never told me?"

"I wasn't allowed to tell anyone, it was covered up by "God" and the Old. Daniel made a gesture that was strange to Michael.

"Why did you do that with your hands and fingers? What does that mean?"

"Oh, it's something I picked up from the Sapiens-Old … it's a gesture they use when they are being openly sarcastic about what they talk about. It is derived from old writing—something called quotation marks."

"But what does it mean? Why did you use that when you said "God"? Are you saying there is *no God*?"

"Oh, you don't know that, either? Sometimes I feel ashamed you're my son, or at least the one I was "lucky" enough to have. Don't get me wrong, Michael; I love you. I always have. You're my child, after all … but I always felt empty, always felt like there was something missing I could never put my finger on." Daniel stood up, looking out into the dense jungle, where a tiger lurked just outside the window. He reached out to pet the fierce creature behind its ear, and the beast fell to the ground, purring in delight. The tiger looked up at Daniel, playfully pawing as it rolled on its back. Daniel ran his hand over the tiger's stomach, and brightly lit, blue beads of energy dripped down from his fingertips, almost liken neon rain drops. The tiger slowly turned into a small housecat as the energy flowed throughout its entire body; it jumped up into Daniel's arms. "Amanda, sweetheart, come here," he called. "Your grandfather has something for you."

She stopped playing with what Michael couldn't see before— some of the tribesmen had been shrunk to the size of dolls to be used as her toys. He cringed in disgust. She'd left them to get her new toy and they ran off screaming, hiding inside her dollhouse.

"Awww ... it's so cute! What's its name?" She looked at Daniel, giving no further thought to the small villagers.

"That's up to you, darling." He handed her the cat to hold. "Now run along and take your toys and go play in the other room for me, won't you, angel?"

"Okay. I think I'm going to name it Chable, as in, 'He's my cat, Chable' ... Anyway, bye, Daddy!! I hope you have as much fun as I'm having. Why didn't you ever tell me the Machine of Forever was so much fun before? Hey, that makes me wonder, are you a program, too, or are you really here?"

Michael started to answer, but Daniel quickly said, "He's really here, sweetheart, but not for long. He's going back home to start dinner for us after he tests out his new invention."

"Oh, okay. Well, this is so much fun I don't ever want to leave!" She kissed them both, grabbed the dollhouse, ignoring the screams of the miniaturized people trapped inside, and ran off into the other room, the cat following the screams of the tempting-looking villagers.

Daniel spoke in the native language of the people, ordering everyone to leave the room but the three guards. The two women holding fans that were standing by his throne scurried out along with the food bearer. The two guards looked at each other and smiled, locking the door. The one guard by the throne looked around nervously, but maintained his position.

"So innocent, she is, and so loved by everyone. Wouldn't you say, Michael?" Daniel turned his back to his son, motioning to the guard to come closer to him. The guard took a deep breath, stepping closer, but not as close as Daniel wanted him. Frustrated, Daniel reached out and pulled him closer with his fist behind the man's neck and, with the other hand, slapped his face. Michael struggled to stand and help the man, but he was still too weak. "What do you think innocence *is,* Michael? Do you think this man is innocent?"

"I have no idea, Father; innocent of what?"

"Innocent of what," Daniel mocked, "innocent of murder, Michael. Innocent of murder!"

"Yes, then. I think he is innocent of murder." Michael stared as the chair he was on sprouted leather straps that wound around his wrists and ankles, binding him fast. His nano-bots failed to respond. *The straps must not be recognized as a threat; how could this be?* he thought. Struggling to free himself, Michael felt a jolt of energy course through his body, paralyzing him, leaving his once-fluent nano-bots now frozen in place and stiff, like the body of a Sapiens-Old. They were unable to break apart like they normally would when sensing incoming danger, a self-defense mechanism given to the Modiens by God. No, this chair, or whatever it was, was blocking that ability. Michael was scared.

"Careful, child. That is very dangerous for us Modified-Sapiens. The current can kill a Modien like us ten times over; even at the lower level it's set on now."

"What is this, Father? Why are you doing this to me?"

"Ah, such a beautifully inquisitive mind we have, don't you think? We always want to know more, more, more! That will come in handy soon. But, to answer your first question.... The device you're in is called an "electric chair." I found the invention and many other interesting machines from the days of the Old during a recent excavation I went on. Does that satisfy your curiosity, or shall I continue?"

Michael struggled again to escape only to be jolted again, forced back to the seat, momentarily stunned. "Why do you do this to me? What have I ever done to you?"

"Nothing, my boy, nothing at all, but I'm sure that won't make you feel any better about me, the situation you're in, or the fact that Amanda has changed from an innocent and beautiful young lady into a murdering puppet of mine."

"What do you mean, murdering? She hasn't killed anyone, nor will she ever!"

Daniel laughed and continued, "I'm sure just the thought of that has to weigh on your mind, right? By the way, how's Marilyn? Remember how you two met? *I* do." He laughed louder and turned his attention back to the guard, who was shivering in place and frozen in fear. "This man you claim to be so innocent is far from innocent; he has killed many people under my order. I've even seen him kill of his own accord. You have no experience of judging what innocence is—no Modien *really* does. I plan to change that, though.

"Not just for you, Michael; you're not *that special* to me, even though you *are* my *only* surviving child," he said in disgust. "I plan to take your precious, loving, caring, and adored family from you, just how they took my wife and first-born child from me.

"Don't worry, though, Michael, Marilyn will be just fine, for now. Well, maybe not *completely* fine. She will wonder what has happened to you; you know, for being gone for so long, not seen by anyone. She'll also have to deal with the fact that I'm back, alive in the real world, and that I'm going to take Amanda under my wing and nurture what's building up inside her right now and what's developed me into the perfect being."

"The perfect being," scoffed Michael. "You think you're perfect?"

"Oh, but I am, my son. Don't you see? Not only do I have superior intelligence that far exceeds any species I've met, but I've done something they haven't: escape death and overthrown this so-called 'God' that supposedly created everything in this universe. I'll get everyone to question his powers and authority over us once I pick and choose who will be on my side and who will suffer my wrath.

"And, if you do escape from here and somehow see your wife again, she'll wonder why you don't remember her and where your love for her has gone, because you won't remember the feelings you have for her. Then, after those precious few minutes when you two finally think you're going to move on with your lives and create a new love for each other, I'll take Marilyn's life. Then you'll know what the emptiness feels like, and it will be a slow, gradual lesson, I'll make sure of that. One that will take centuries for you to fully understand what it is that you could have done to deserve such a punishment. Only I'm sparing you the full pain that was given to me, like the memory I have leftover of completely losing not only my wife, Jessica, but my unborn son, Jeremiah. I'm sparing you the full emptiness that I felt, losing the child I cared about more than anything in the world.

"No, my son; I'll spare you Amanda's life, but the loss of Marilyn will feel like your soul is crumbling in a forever-deepening hole nevertheless." Daniel looked at the guard again and caressed his cheek. A green wave of energy rippled through the flesh and coursed throughout his body along the path of his veins. A few seconds later, the man was frozen solid as stone, looking like a statue in the palace, looking like the other stone statues of people frozen in various positions. Daniel raised his hands toward the front of the newly formed statue, and it slid across the floor next to the others that had been lined up. He spoke to the other two guards, and they ran out of the room. "Innocent," he boasted. "You will surely know what that means soon enough. Now, are you *sure* you want the answer to the question as to *why* I'm doing this?" Daniel asked.

"What do you think, *Dad?*" Michael replied in the same sarcastic tone.

"The 'why' really makes no difference to me, Michael; that's something you will have to figure out on your own, and you will have plenty of time to do so, too, for I'm leaving you here as I take Amanda out into the real world. Only I won't be as cruel to you as 'God' was to me by killing *both of my loved ones*, you should be thankful for that. But I *will* erase the rest of the memories you have of Amanda and Marilyn, leaving you to only remember them as these two amazing beings you had in your life once, and wanting to be with them again. All you will remember when you look at pictures of them is how you were once married to this wonderful, amazing wife Marilyn. How you once had this amazingly gifted child, Amanda.... You *will* experience the emptiness that I have had since I found out that I had lost my loved ones and you will keep that emptiness for eternity. You're going to suffer the same fate as I am suffering now. Please, believe that it is not because I like seeing you suffer, my child—I'm not that cold-hearted. No, it's because I have so much hate for the suffering that was thrust upon me, that has been brewing for centuries inside me, only now to come to head and morph into my wonderful plan of revenge.

"I already know Amanda has wiped out much of the memory you have of Marilyn, but not all of it. She was told to leave what was important. You know, for your lesson."

"You can't be serious, Father! Look at what you're doing, here! You're in charge, here. You're the one that can stop this now. Release me, Father. It's the right thing to do."

Daniel started laughing louder, totally ignoring Michael's pleas. He waved his hand around at the exterior wall of the stone building. Bolts of white lightning crackled from his fingertips, and the light slowly dissolved the wall away, exposing the village and jungle in the background, and the squawks of the birds in the distance could be heard. "Now, Michael, you know I can't do that. If I were to release you now, how would we react around each other from now on? I mean, it would be a little awkward, don't you think? What are we supposed to do, reminisce about I held you hostage, and didn't tell your daughter to set you free while at the same time helping with *her* plan to exact revenge on the person that is actually responsible for all of this: "God"? Do you think we could laugh about this one day? No, my son, this has to be. Your daughter gave me the courage to stand up for what I believe in; she gave me the motivation to get this revenge."

"Don't be ridiculous; she would never come up with such a plan!"

"Oh, she did, my son, and I was so happy to see her that first time she came in here without you. It was so amazing to see the look on her face when she found out all the things she could do inside here. The second time she came in, she was slightly different. She was more curious than I've ever seen her, Michael. I have never heard such questions, either."

Michael listened to how his daughter was the one that actually broke the rules, being under the age of 10 and going inside the Machine of Forever without a parent. He listened to how his daughter had transformed from this pure little girl into this murderous monster. It made him sick.

Daniel continued, "She asked me all about her Grandmother Jessica and how she'd died. It was funny … it was almost like she was there, the way she was talking to me. She would bring up details that she couldn't have known. Details that only I knew after finding out what the actual cause of my wife's death was. Amanda somehow knew it was the surge of power that killed Jessica.

"She felt such compassion for me, Michael, she cried, and held me as I cried. She told me how sorry she was that all of that had happened and mentioned how wonderful it would be for me to have my Jessica back. She told me she could bring her back to me, back in my arms and in my life again. All I had to do was help her, Michael. I just wanted my Jessica back—you can understand that, can't you? I mean, you can understand how I..." but before Daniel finished that sentence, he realized that his son really didn't understand. He didn't really know what it was like to lose a wife. "No, you don't understand, but you will. I will teach you and everyone."

"Teach us what, Father?"

Daniel smiled, then called for the two guards that had left just moments before. They came running up to his side again after having gathered all the villagers. At Daniel's request, they had told them that if they came right away, their God would reward them with riches beyond their imagination.

Daniel walked out to the ledge, speaking out to the crowd. "The moment of truth is upon you; only the strong will survive. All those who follow me now, and those who survive will have power, riches, land with fertile soil, and long, healthy lives." The whole village shouted and cheered for Daniel. He looked over back at Michael and shouted out, "The essence of innocence, Michael, what else?" Daniel told the people to prepare for the battle ahead asking only for their loyalty, for which he would reward them beyond their wildest dreams. He threw gold coins out to them; the crowd shouted and cheered again, then dispersed to their houses to prepare for battle.

"You see, my dear boy, I have found a way to no longer be trapped inside this "heaven" of mine. The Ball of Essence will no longer contain me, for my "heaven" has grown, with my desire, in scope. I shall be reborn in eyes of the New Earth; everyone will love me again as they did before I passed on. I will be like a God to them, like I am already God here.

"I shall rise from the dead, spreading a message of hope, promising no one else will ever die again. Of course, this will be a lie. I won't bring back *everyone;* no, I'll just bring back enough for them to believe in me and my powers. And when they see my powers, they will believe anything I say, and I'll tell them how "God" has lied to all of us about who He really is and how He kept it from them. I'll tell His lies for Him, since He was too much of a coward to tell everyone Himself. I'll tell them everything, Michael; I'll tell them how He murdered my wife and unborn son, His true identity, how He is no different from us."

"No one will care, Father, just like you didn't care when you first heard it from Him. What makes you believe they will think differently?"

"They will have no choice, my boy."

"Don't be ridiculous! Everyone has a choice. They're smart enough and compassionate enough to see that if He is like us, then He, too, can make mistakes. After all, you forgave Him at first."

"Yes, I did. A mistake I won't make again, but that was then and this is now. And now, not only has my view changed about Him, but with my newest and best invention, everyone's view will change about Him, too. They will drink from the Stream of Life, as I call it, thinking that by doing so they will bring their loved ones back. What it will really do is switch off the genes in their DNA that produce love and compassion, changing them into greedy, selfish individuals caring only for what suits their needs best."

"You're a monster! What could possibly be gained by our society to bring back those dark forces?"

"How do you know that bringing them back won't do any good? How can you be sure that if I introduce those practices and ways of the Old into the Modified-Sapiens society that something bad will come from it? Our people will know that life isn't always perfect, that there is real suffering going on. They will learn how to cope with all the hardships that have been forgotten for nearly a thousand years, and been told to not look at the suffering of their Sapiens-Old while in their A.T.M.'s. They will learn how to deal with others better by understanding their true identity, rather than this modified personality we've had for so long. Everyone will see each other for what they really are; their true characters will be determined. Instead of this "everything's great" and "there's no such thing as bad or evil" mentality that is the way of society now, everything will change forever, for the better."

Michael, although not nearly as smart as he was since his daughter attacked him and wiped out much of his memory, still remembered the Switch and responded with, "Don't you understand, though, Father, that those practices and ways of the Old were *already* considered bad for our life, and that's *why* Modiens were designed the way they were? To block as much of those genes in our DNA as possible? There is nothing that can be learned by bringing back evil, Father. You must reconsider this course. Why go back to a system that has already failed? Give up."

Daniel chuckled to himself, retorting in a studious tone, "Michael, when you were young and I brought you to the Museum of Ages, do you remember seeing something called a 'stove'?"

"Yes, but..."

"Remember how I told you how the Old would cook food on this thing, and that it got very hot and not to touch it because you would burn yourself, and then you touched it anyway?

Michael remembered the pain, but he was still confused. "What's your point, Dad? I touched it anyway and got burned. You want to see the rest of humanity get burned by trying the ways you're bringing back?"

"Well, maybe not *burned* actually, and maybe that, too, but that's not the important part. I want them to touch it out of *curiosity*. I want them to learn new things about themselves. I want to control their thoughts and actions and *make them see and feel* what I have. I want them to experience the pain that I have, and when they've had enough, I'll tell them whose fault it really is. GOD. They will side with me, and along with the Mysorians, we ALL shall overthrow this imposter and reclaim our rightful spot in the universe, as supreme beings, and I will be their leader. I'll make God suffer in realizing He is not perfect and that His "perfect" creation has turned against Him; He will be living in a cage by the time I'm done with Him!"

"You will never succeed, Father. You will perish. God created us. Don't you think if He really wanted to, He could destroy you?"

"How could He? I've come back from death; what more could He do? He could even disperse my body throughout the entire universe, every piece of me, and I'd still return. You know why? Because I can, Michael. I know more than ever; escaping this 'heaven' of mine has opened up new trains of thought, new connections, and I realize my true potential, and I won't let anyone stop it, not you, and not a lying, fraudulent being no better than I!"

"You're no better than, Satan, Father."

"Nevertheless, Amanda has inspired me to do her bidding, to take revenge for what has been done to me, and she will give back the one true thing I ever wanted in my life, Jessica's love for me. It's perfect, you see; Amanda and her popularity will rev up our plans to spread our ideas to the farthest reaches of the known universe, a new way of living that Modiens won't be able to resist. Among other things, they will learn what is innocent and what isn't."

"How do you plan to do that, Father?"

Daniel pointed to the man he'd just frozen into stone a few moments earlier. "The same way you learned what innocence was, my boy; you learned this man isn't innocent of murder because *I* told you he had killed. The Modiens will learn innocence from people they've killed, or haven't … or from learning whatever else that has been kept from us from our beginning … it's really up to them to learn what they want to learn, you see." Daniel freed Michael from the electric chair and called out for Amanda to come back in, and for her to bring her toys.

She ran in, holding the huge dollhouse that was slightly bigger than she and was filled with the tiny people. "Yes, Grandpa?" She set down her toy.

"What would you say your daddy is missing, angel?"

Without hesitation, she answered, "Innocence, Grandpa. I can feel it now."

"That's right, angel, and how can you feel his lack of innocence?" Daniel smirked with delight at the upcoming answer.

"Because I found *my* innocence…. Why?"

"Your father wants to know why innocence is such an important thing to learn about, that's why. And tell Daddy how you *lost* your innocence. You're going to love this, son."

"Well, you see, once I got the idea to make a fake M.E.T. to see Grandpa, I went to the Building of Souls and tried to get the help of some woman, who was leaving after visiting her relative. Only…." She stopped to think about how it had happened.

"Only what, angel? What'd you do to that woman?"

"Only she started to question where *you* were. After I said that you told me to go in first, that you'd be right along in a couple minutes, she said she was going to report me to the Sentinel of Souls. I just couldn't have let that happen, Daddy." She stopped again. In a somber tone, as though she regretted having done what she was about to tell her father she'd done, she said, "I just touched her, Daddy; I swear. The next thing I knew she started to completely disappear!"

"Amanda, baby, please … Daddy wants us to go home now … stop this foolishness and show me the way home. Please?" Michael was in complete denial now, thinking she was making it all up; she'd never kill anyone.

"You're wasting your time, Michael; she's having too much fun learning the new things she can do inside an A.T.M., aren't you Amanda?"

"Oh, yes! Daddy, I still can't believe you never told me how much fun you can have inside one of these things! I would always hear stories about how you would give all these incredible inventions to your Sapiens-Old, always making me think of the inventions I'd give *my* Sapiens Old. Now I get my chance!"

"You sure do, Amanda. Now tell your Daddy how you felt once you lost your innocence."

"It felt like nothing I could describe before. When I found out that that woman had *died* after I touched her, and that it was so *wrong* … it felt *amazing*. It felt so … natural." She stopped to savor thinking about that feeling, and the corner of her mouth broke out in a little grin. "I want that feeling for *everyone*, Daddy. And, with Grandpa's help, I will rule the universe, spreading that wonderful feeling for everyone to appreciate. They will learn innocence, they will learn so many new things, Daddy, and you can't believe what *we* will learn."

"But, baby, that's not innocence! That's evil! You are feeling the seductive power of evil!!! Grandpa has been lying to you to get you to serve his twisted revenge needs! There is a reason we have to wait until we turn 18 before we're allowed to operate our own A.T.M. Your mind is just too young to handle the ways of the Sapiens-Old. They're more susceptible to evil; Satan's powers have more sway over their species … even our *young* minds are really too weak to stand up to his powers. Once we turn 10, though, certain genes inside the Heart Collection start to activate and get produced more than the other side of the genes. There's a reason why we, the Modified-Sapiens, are made this way, to make sure the evil part of our genes stay dormant. *And Grandpa is activating yours.*"

"So I won't have my own Sapiens-Old until I'm 18, now? That's not what Grandpa told me … you're just trying to keep me from having one now," Amanda said petulantly, picking.

"No, Amanda! It's different where life and evil are simulated, not like an A.T.M. where you're dealing with real live beings. Amanda, you have to trust me. You're not emotionally mature enough to understand it or to make good choices. We have to leave here at once! Now let me out!"

"Enough!" shouted Daniel. "It's too late to reason with her, Michael. She loves me and sympathizes with me for my suffering. She has plans for the future of our race and for all the races of the universe. Don't you get it, son? You said it yourself, 'There's nothing like the experience you get with actually working on what you're trying to learn….' Now you can't tell Amanda that it's okay to only learn certain things and forget the rest, can you, son?"

Michael sat silently.

"And with that, Amanda, show Daddy something I taught you." He called out for the people to assemble once again. They quickly obeyed, running out of their houses. He told them how lucky they were to be in the presence of such a gifted child. To worship her, for she will bring them a life they couldn't have imagined before. They shouted and chanted her name, waiting for her to show herself to them.

She put down the cat and shrank it, giving it to the people in the dollhouse. She walked over in front of the line of frozen people and smiled. She pointed at the line of statues and blue sparks beamed across the room and over the first statue, melting away the stone, exposing the being inside. The sparks spread throughout the line, one by one changing the stone back into human beings. Once the people inside were all turned back, they realized no harm had been done to them, and they saw their loved ones and friends cheering for them and for what Amanda had done. They bowed to her and chanted her name.

Daniel told everyone who witnessed it how lucky they were to be in the presence of such a remarkable being. "Wonderful job, Amanda, my love—you're so good at this. See how everyone loves you?"

Michael, frozen in awe and disgust, looked around frantically, trying to think of a way to escape and somehow stop Daniel. He had no idea, though, what Daniel's powers were inside here. He was out of ideas about how to convince Amanda how wrong this was, and that it was not too late to stop. She might not even care how wrong it was just to have that feeling she'd felt. It scared him to his core.

"Daddy, see what I did? I made life! I created Sapiens-Old! I turned stone into people! Isn't that amazing? Oh, Grandpa, I'm having so much fun inside your A.T.M! Look at all the people—they're all so happy with what I can do!" Amanda boasted, not knowing she'd only turned the people *back* from stone, that she hadn't really created life itself at all.

"I know, dear, I know," Daniel answered again for Michael. "Soon, everyone will be happy. And remember the best part: any time we spend in an A.T.M. is only five minutes outside in the New Earth. Let's try your new skills in a city, and we can come back here later. Gather your things while I talk to your father."

"Wow, really? This is so much fun; are there lots of statues in the city? I can't wait!"

"There are lots of statues, and while we're walking to the city, I can teach you some new things you can try out on the people. Sound fun?"

"Yes! I can't believe this is happening! I've dreamt of this for so long, and now I can actually play inside an A.T.M.!"

"That's right, angel, fun in the sun." Daniel turned his attention to the people and told them to rejoice, enjoy their time with each other, and to get ready for the battle ahead. Once again they scurried back to their homes, chanting their war-cry. Daniel quickly materialized a new wall around the three of them. "Now, there aren't as many statues in the city, at least not in one place, but how about you try *making* statues?"

Her face lit up. "Can I *really* do that? What would I have to do?"

"Well, remember how I told you to think about making a Sapiens-Old just by thinking the statue was a person?"

"Uh huh. Do I just think about making people into statues, and they'll become so?"

"That's right, angel; you're so smart. And, don't you worry— remember they're just programs in my A.T.M., so they won't mind. Their atoms will just rematerialize into other pieces to build other things; they won't feel a thing."

"Amanda, no! He's ly—"

Daniel quickly silenced him by sealing his mouth closed with a loose strap from the electric chair. "Awww, Michael, what's wrong, my son? Is it your new invention? I know how that goes. I had many unexpected setbacks working on some of my inventions. Why, once I even had all my nano-bots get disassembled while working on the A.T.M. Luckily my Vial of Viability was protected from the impact from falling out of my body, unlike what happened to my wife. Anyway, Amanda, go run along and play with your dollhouse for a few minutes while I talk to your father, okay?"

"Yay! Okay, Grandpa. Hurry, though—I want to try making statues as soon as I can!" She skipped out of the room, singing in delight.

"You think I'm evil. You see, being the first Modified-Sapiens ever, I had the first Modified-Sapiens *wife* ever. And, after the rest of the other Modiens were made from the DNA of the Old, Jessica and I were to have the first Modified-Sapiens child ever. Are you following?" Well, the Old and God were very excited indeed. They were all wondering how the procedure would work, creating the very first offspring of the Modified-Sapiens species. As you already know, it didn't go very well. Jessica and I arrived at the Essence Accumulating Center to pick the DNA for Jeremiah. There were only the two of us, some members of the Old, and God. He is, for all I have gathered, someone that has been around for a very long time, much longer than any Modien or member of the Old has been. And he created THIS universe that we live in, that much I know."

"Okay," Michael answered, wondering where this was going.

"But, think about it. How different is He *really* from us? WE create universes for Homo sapiens to live in. What is the difference, because we call them "Sapiens-Old" instead of

Homo sapiens? They *are* Homo sapiens, Michael, just like the Old.

"And then, there is the conversation." Daniel paused, the light of mania gone from his face. "One day shortly after I was created, I overheard Him talking to two members of the Old while I came in for my daily check-up. He was saying to them, "*HE* will be pleased at what *I'VE* accomplished by making a new race of human beings. I wonder what *HE* will think of them once *I* come back with HIM after I leave." I didn't hear any more, since the workers came into the room after that. I pretended I hadn't heard a thing, and they went on with the check-up. I had heard it, though. Who was God talking about? Who was 'HE? ' Who would God have to impress or please? Whoever this higher being was, I wondered years later if He had known how God had failed, how God had killed Jessica and Jeremiah. You'd think if He *were God* He wouldn't have made *that* mistake now would 'HE? ' And, what convinced me finally that God was a fraud was the fact that He had a superior being to which He would be held accountable. One cannot be omniscient and have a boss. No, God was not God at all."

Michael was perplexed. He had nothing to defend himself or God with. He wondered why the being he had always known as God would keep such a secret from the Modiens. Why would He cover up how the Modien Essence Extraction Device had killed the first person it was used on? Why lie about that? What would He have to gain by not telling the truth? Then he thought how *he, himself, Michael,* really wasn't *that* different from *God.* God had his Modiens and his Sapiens-Old inside the universe that HE'D created, just like Michael had his very own species inside *his* universe. "I really am like God...."

"Do you know what happened to those members of the Old that God had that conversation with?"

Michael said nothing.

"Within weeks, they were the first ones to die, out of the hundreds of thousands of the Old. A little odd, don't you think? Especially considering how much *longer* all the *rest of the other members* lived. Interesting isn't it?"

"What about the Bible, Dad?"

"What about it?" He responded curtly.

"Everything came true that was written in it. It even says God had a son in the Bible! What if God was just talking about his son when you overheard him talking to the Old?"

"I don't buy it. It's just too convenient. Most of the Old don't even know the bit of information I'm about to tell you, Michael, but I know you won't tell anyone. Jessica and I were told that the whole thing would only take a few minutes, and at the end of it we'd have a beautiful new baby boy. We couldn't have been happier, it seemed. A few of the Old took her off into another room. She was going to have her DNA extracted first. A couple of the Old stayed with me as I waited for my turn. I was so excited, so very excited. I felt that, after all the time I'd spent just being developed as the first-ever Modified-Sapiens, this was the best possible reward I ever could have imagined." A tear escaped his eye, but Daniel didn't notice, he continued as though in a trance. "When they came out, I knew something was wrong. They told me when they tried to take the DNA out of Jessica's Vial of Viability using the Modien Essence Extraction Device, her circuits started overloading. They told me her nano-bots, which kept her Vial of Viability safe inside her, started to lose their bonds with each other because their electrical circuitry was shorting out. They said her Vial of Viability crashed to the ground and shattered before anyone could react. Once the vial broke, the rest of the nano-bots started crumbling completely apart, falling to the floor. They told me it hadn't hurt and that she had died quickly." Daniel stood up and walked over to the window. "They said they'd make it up to me, offering me a new wife and child. They said they could even make Jessica just the way she was. I didn't want any part of it. I vowed then and there to get some sort of retribution for what they'd done. I didn't know how or when, but I knew deep down that I would. I'm just sorry it has to be you and Amanda. I never had the heart for revenge before, though, Michael...." Daniel waved over the Flying Food Fabricator he'd recreated for his heaven, put his hand inside, and out popped a s'mores. "Here you go, my child. I know these are your favorite. Try to relax here in my heaven—you will be here a while."

For some odd reason, Michael took the s'mores. He felt defeated and bewildered, but started eating anyway. It comforted him, despite everything. "So, after 650 years of doing what you have always done, trying to make the perfect society and creating relations with other civilizations, you decided to have me." Michael thinks some more. "You said for all that time before you had me, you didn't have the heart. What's changed?"

"Oh, Michael. I don't know who should tell you. Should she tell you, or should I? You won't believe me though, if I tell you." Daniel forced Michael back into the electric chair and strapped him in. "This won't be easy for you, my boy. Amanda, angel, Daddy wants to ask you something. Come in here, please."

"You're a monster! She isn't the one that came up with this! I don't believe you!"

"Yes, Daddy? Hey, why are you in that chair?"

"Never mind that, now; Amanda, your father has something he wants to know. He doesn't believe me when I tell him, so I figured he would believe it from you."

"Baby, it's very important that you tell me the truth when I ask you this, okay?"

"Okay, Daddy. Anything for you."

Michael took a deep breath to prepare himself for the worst, not knowing just how bad it really was. "Amanda, I know you love Grandpa, and I know how much you've wanted to have your very own A.T.M., but whose idea was it for you to come in here?"

Amanda giggled again. "Oh, Daddy! You always ask such silly questions!"

"Stop laughing and answer me, Amanda. This is serious!"

Amanda's face turned quickly from glee and excitement to fright. With a scowl she answered, almost defiantly, "It was my idea. I figured out a way to get inside without you. I wanted to see him more and you never want to take me."

Michael sat in disbelief. "But how'd you come up with such an idea? Why'd you want to come inside here without me to begin with?"

"Well, Father, if you must know, I got the idea one day walking Brody. And I wanted to come in here to see Grandpa. Happy?"

"The idea to bring back evil the likes of which haven't been seen since the days of the Old? That's the idea *you* came up with? I don't believe it."

"Oh, trust me, Daddy. It was I that wanted a change from what's going on today."

"So you were just walking around with Brody one day and got the idea to avenge Daniel and to bring back a new way of evil? Am I understanding this correctly? Is there anything else you want to tell me?"

"Like what? What else do you want to know, Daddy? I'll tell you anything you want. I have nothing to hide," she looked over at Daniel. "Not like God, right, Grandpa?"

"That's right, angel, you tell him."

"I want to know where you were walking Brody, Amanda. I find it hard to believe you got such a strange and terrifying idea on your own, while simply doing something you've done hundreds of times. Now tell me the truth!"

"I *am*, Daddy, only...."

"Only *what*?"

"Only ... Brody pulled me by the Pother and ... I looked inside."

"No, no, no baby! Say it isn't true!" Michael hung his head. It all made sense now. Satan had gotten to Amanda.

"What's the big deal, Daddy? I only looked inside for a few seconds. It wasn't such a big deal—fun, but nothing special. I saw you, Mom, and Brody all at the beach. We were having so much fun, it seemed. We were all laughing. Then...."

"Then what happened, baby?"

"I don't know, Daddy. I remember all of us at the beach and laughing, then the next thing I remember I was just walking through the crowd with Brody, on our way home again."

"Is that when you go the idea, though, Amanda?"

"Kind of, but first I got the idea to go see Grandpa by myself. It didn't seem like the wrong thing to do at all. It was easy; I just figured out a way to copy your DNA once I had the blueprints to make a Modien Essence Transmitter. I calculated the DNA you have from the DNA that I have, figuring that most of mine would be very much like yours—after all, we are so much alike. Once I made DNA strands that were exactly like yours, I made an M.E.T. that's also an exact copy of yours."

"But how'd you get the material to even make the M.E.T.? That material was made by God. No one has ever been able to replicate it before."

"Michael," Daniel interrupted them, "do you remember that man's invention you saw on the sidewalk one day after work? Well, it was the funniest thing; the man that invented that came to visit me just days before Amanda came in to see me. He showed me that amazing invention of his and even said I could use it in here, giving me the blueprints to build my own."

"So," Michael interrupted his father for once, "what's that got to do with Amanda getting the material to build a M.E.T.?"

"After obtaining the blueprints for that memory machine, I created one of my own, one that works whenever someone comes to visit me. That memory machine is quite a marvel of engineering, I must say. The scanner reads every atom of the Modien that is going to be traveling inside the machine itself."

"So?"

"So, it actually has to scan what the Modien Essence Transmitter is made of to recreate the memories of the person that's traveling through the machine. I convinced the man to let Amanda take his ride, and I implanted the idea for the blueprints in her mind. The hard part was the wait to see if she could actually make a fake M.E.T. I just wanted to see Amanda more, Michael. This plan for the New Earth is all hers. But do I love it! Ask her; she'll say she went through it."

"Did you, baby? Did you go through that memory machine?"

"I sure did, Daddy. I was sure happy to see Grandpa again. I always wanted to see him more, but you always said "soon." Well, it wasn't soon enough for me."

"You see, Michael? It was her idea to come in here. I just nudged her a bit by telling that man to make sure she got through the memory machine. All he had to do was lure her inside. That was easy, as you know all too well, don't you, Michael? It lured you in quite easily."

"How'd you come up with this plan to change the world then, Amanda?"

"After I came in here and I saw Grandpa, he told me all that has happened to him. I didn't think it was fair that Grandma Jessica died at all. I felt so sad for Grandpa that I had to help him. He and I left the second time I came back, after I went inside the Pother. While in the outside world, he showed me this place from the time of the Old that he had just discovered. It had all these writings and information on how people used to behave before the Apocalypse...."

"That's enough, Amanda." Daniel quieted her by patting her on the shoulder. "Oh Michael, how dumbstruck you must be right now. Didn't see this coming, did you? Here you thought this whole time *I* was the monster when it was your own daughter all along."

"But how did you leave here, Father? How did you figure out a way to get back in the outside world again, to become a living Modien again? How can you leave the Building of Souls? No one can leave once they pass on—it's impossible."

"Oh, Michael, you're disappointing me more and more. So naïve. I wouldn't be doing all this if I *couldn't leave* the Building of Souls. Have you been listening at all? *I* was the *first Modien EVER!* I know everything there is to know about A.T.M.s and certainly know about the Building of Souls. I was the one that created the first A.T.M., me! I know how they operate from the inside out, which is exactly how I'm leaving here. I'll tell you the method of how I escaped. It's a program that I've created, one that links the inside of this "heaven" of mine to the outside world. This program runs through the stream in this jungle, which is on one of your planets, actually. Don't you recognize where we are?"

"But how did you even know about this place? I never told you about it; you couldn't have gone into my A.T.M. to find this place."

"I didn't have to go inside your A.T.M. to get that information. *You* gave me that information when you came inside here not too long ago. Remember? It was after Jacob saw Doctor Kimberly for the first time and you came to see me and asked me what I remember of colds."

"But why this place, Dad? What's so special about the first civilization I ever created? Why not use one of the thousands of civilizations you kept? What possible advantage would you have by using?"

"What difference does it make, Michael? But if you must know, I used your civilization because it was connected to the outside; my civilizations are all trapped inside the Ball of Essence. If you think you can leave here just by following the stream, you're sorely wrong; that will just have you walking through my heaven. It won't lead you outside where I'm going. And while on the outside, I shall help Amanda establish the plans we have for the New Earth."

Michael said, mostly to himself, "I should have seen it coming—I should have known from my visions...."

"Again, what difference does it make now? It's in the past. Let's just say we both did things we regret. Oh, and Amanda, remind me to thank Zandessa and her grandson for helping me out with that wonderful invention of his. I keep forgetting to give credit where credit is due. Must have picked that up from HIM."

Michael shook his head; he wasn't even thinking of that aspect of all of this, but it suddenly came to him. "Why did that man help you out?" He blurted out of nowhere. "Who is he?" He thought back to his days of school, and he remembered seeing that same man as a kid in his class when he was growing up, but his name escaped him.

"It's coming back to you now isn't it? Amanda will have to work on her memory-erasing skills. That man is a grandson of a member of the Old, Zandessa. She and I have a special relationship. She used to be quite fond of me and I was fond of her, even though we were two completely different species. Love knows no boundaries. Anyway, it was a couple of years after I lost Jessica that we met. She told me that she had deep sympathy for me and felt that what I went through was just horrible, and after that we had become close friends. She said she'd help someday if I ever needed it.

"And once it was my time to pass on, she was very vocal in my defense, saying I should not die, no one should. She fought hard for immortality of all, and many agreed with her. But the powers that be had spoken. I, like the rest of the Modiens that were to turn 800, were to be recycled. Condemned to the Machine of Forever, at least that's how I saw it. For everyone else, though, it's amazing. Even more amazing than being a Modien, but it isn't heaven for me. It's hell for me, Michael, and I feel I have suffered long enough for something that wasn't supposed to be. I've suffered long enough for God and His mistakes."

"Amanda, baby. Listen to Daddy. Please. You're too good for this, angel. These things you've been doing. They're evil. Killing! It's not a game. You've had your fun inside an A.T.M., now let's go home. Say goodbye to Grandpa."

"Sorry, Daddy, I have seen what needs to be brought back to the human race … fear."

"Why, though, baby? Why do you want to bring back what God fought so hard to get rid of for us?"

"Because, Daddy, it's what I do best. Besides, I've always felt sorry for Grandpa, that it wasn't fair of God to let Jessica die like that. I saw it all, and I wanted to do something then, but I couldn't. Now I can."

"What are you talking about, sweetheart? This is crazy!"

It hit him, suddenly. Michael knew he was not talking to his daughter anymore, but to Satan, whose powers started building again from within her, from her brief time inside the Pother. "You think this is crazy, Daddy? That's weird. You see, just as I have looked at the Pother and now have some of his powers coursing through me, with Grandpa's invention, they won't have to look at the Pother to have their evil genes activated inside their Vial of Viability, and the Pother will transfigure from the mist it is now into their very souls. Their DNA will begin to subtly change how they think and feel. It will do all this through the program Grandpa Daniel invented to link his heaven to the outside world of the New Earth. "

Michael said, mostly to himself, "I should have seen it coming—I should have known from my visions...."

"What difference does it make now my son? It's in the past. Let's just say we both did things we regret. This is supposed to be heaven, but it isn't for me. It's hell for me, Michael, and I feel I have suffered long enough for something that wasn't supposed to be. I've suffered long enough for God and his mistakes."

"But you have that love of Jessica back now, why go through with ... the ... her ... plans at all?"

"Because, my son, I don't want what happened to me to happen to anyone else, ever. I will expose Him for the liar He is, the ultimate con artist that He is. I will tear down His reputation of being infallible and all loving. I'll tell my true story, the one He had covered up. Why, I even forgot to tell you the best part of it all, what He did to those members of the Old."

"Let me guess, He killed them too, right? What's to say you're not lying to me now, Dad?"

"Pretty smart my boy, even for having the I.Q. of a Sapiens-Old now."

Michael was becoming increasingly confused, and he wasn't sure if it was his damaged brain or that his father's arguments were starting to take root. He still did not fully understand how things *really* were right after the Apocalypse. And how God was working with the Old to make the new species of the human race. Did He in fact cover up Jessica's death by killing off those two members of the Old? He never fully understood how every action in his life was recorded, for that matter. He never questioned much … there was no need. That after he passed on, his life would be inserted inside the Machine of Forever. The only difference for the Modien that's alive and one that's passed on is that the dead *are* in fact *caged* inside the Machine of Forever. Their memories are floating around in a fixed space, randomly, as a huge ball of energy, inside a room. The only time they are to be assembled at all is when AND IF a family member wants to visit. Once they do decide to see their relatives, they first start the visit going through another cage … the Machine of Forever. Michael thought how lonely the dead must be since only his or her family can come and see them, but no one else. How the dead have to rely on their memories to reproduce the lives they once had.

Daniel was still blathering on. "I'll use my celebrity, and the fact I conquered death to become immortal, to spread our wonderful plans of forgotten ways. Forgotten ways that leave our souls empty of the full potential of life, the absolute necessity of life, which our society has been missing from the start, and that's evil. The lack of it has been stymieing our growth as a species and denying our true nature."

Michael laughed this time. "Our true nature? You're saying our true nature is to have evil in our lives?"

"Yes, my boy. For without it, how would we know what good really is?"

"Because we can feel it, Father, we can feel the goodness we do within, don't you remember that feeling?"

"I remember it all too well. It's what's driving me now. It's what will drive everyone to spread this evil to enlighten everyone as to what they're really feeling."

Again Michael can't help but laugh. "You've got to be kidding me. You're saying you're feeling good about yourself by spreading this evil into our society, and that people will be grateful for this?"

"Amazing, isn't it, son? The very thing that was fought so hard to be exterminated might just be our savior."

"Our savior? How?"

"Our society has been fabricated for too long, and it's time for a change. Our species is slowly becoming sterile. Mindless drones that know nothing of life and the pain it really brings; all they know is how to smile and love, for everything's fine and dandy. Even death is celebrated by us, making it a good thing, a welcomed thing. Well, everything can't be fine and dandy and everyone will learn these new feelings and love them just as I have come to love them. ,

Michael remembered what Jacob said once, how of all the thousand-plus years in his life, he would miss learning new things the most. He never fully understood the depth of that statement until now. Then he thought of Amanda, and her upcoming Big Bang, how excited she got to learn new things. He cringed at the thought, though, of her spreading this newly found evil conjured up by his own father and his discovery of those texts from the times of the Old. How disgusting it all made him feel.

Daniel realized his son was yet again in deep thought so he decided to continue nonetheless. "I've basically come back from the dead … don't you realize what that will mean to people, Michael? The hope that will give them that they, too, will never die…. How I'll bring back every one they ever loved and lost in their lives. I'll raise the dead, Michael, just how I brought myself back. Then everyone will worship me, not the "God" that left us here. Having us experience this incredible life filled with such excitement and knowledge, making us want more of it, for as long as we can. And then when you're just getting used to it all, *HE takes it away from you! Why*, because *HE says so*? Because *HE* knows what's best for *US,* that *WE* don't matter as much as *HIM*? I don't think that's fair! I feel we should NOT die! To NOT be these relics, these obsolete programs of our former lives, disposed of at the living's convenience. To release the restraint were we could no longer grow with ANY knowledge after we pass on. But it won't be for free! I'm going to make sure of that."

Michael remembered again what Jacob said about how he was going to miss learning the most. "How do you know you won't learn anything new when the people stop visiting?"

"Because I've experienced it. I'm sure for most of the Modiens, their experience of heaven, their imagination, quells their thirst for the knowledge life. They are far too busy creating anything and everything they want, oblivious to the fact they have become black holes. All of those black holes, 'living,' as it were, inside the Machine of Forever. Nothing more than energy that takes in information in the form of more energy. And they can do *nothing* with that information; they can't make anything it that can exist outside of the Ball of Essence. In fact, the Ball of Essence is just like a super-massive black hole, a collection of all the other littler black holes it's acquired."

Michael was enraged. "How can you call the Heavenly Coded and the Building of Souls black holes? God gave us the Machine of Forever; He knew how much it hurt the Old when they lost a loved one. He knew the pain involved and *gave US* the Machine of Forever to allow us to *be* with the ones we have loved and lost again. Don't you see how fortunate *we* are? Don't *you* see how much better *our* lives are than *the Old*? Do you know the true reason behind having the Ball of Essence inside the Machine of Forever?"

Daniel's face turned from boastfulness to disgust. "My boy, of course I see how much better *you* have life. But, it seems you fail to see my side. Maybe you will if you ever lose Marilyn. Maybe you will see it when I take everyone you have ever cared about, forever. And you will be stuck here, inside the Machine of Forever, forever. You'll think it's heaven, reliving every wonderful thing you have done in your mere 340 years on the New Earth. You'll only have your memories of Marilyn and Amanda and all the good times, yet you will know that this is it, they're gone forever. You will never see them again once they pass on. You will also know what I am doing on the outside, with your daughter, and potentially to *your* beloved wife, Marilyn. You're going to feel empty, unsure, and unable to do anything about it, much like how I couldn't do a thing about losing Jessica. Much like how *everyone* feels knowing they can *only* see the people they love IF they visit you or if they die. Maybe a couple hundred years isolated from everyone you care about will get you to see *my side.* Maybe by then you will realize that memories can only do so much for the human spirit. Maybe you will see that this 'heaven' of yours created by that *your* precious 'God' is actually a hell, a hell I no longer care to be in. Maybe it will come to you how right I am once you realize you're helpless, stuck in here, while I could be killing everyone you love. Well, not me.... Amanda."

"You monster!"

"Yes. 'God' is, Michael. And HE is the one allowing me to do this. THAT, my boy, is who you can blame for all this. In His absence I shall rule. I will be *the* god everyone will turn to, to look for answers as to what's going on. I'm going to bring it *all* back, all the pain, the sickness, the suffering, the greed and envy, all of it is coming back with a vengeance! And that will be just the start. I'll introduce all the ways of life that the Old thought were detrimental to them. I'll bring back what your 'God' fought so hard to put in a cage all throughout the universe, and all His unique views and practices on life that are now deemed 'unworthy' by our kind."

"And you don't think that there might be a better way to solve your issues with God, Father? You feel sickness and greed and whatever else it is you have planned have any value in the whole scheme of it all? What good could all those things bring to the human experience?"

"You're so naïve, SO NAÏVE! I sometimes feel ashamed you are created from me. You have no imagination, and you have no view of the big picture, you only see what you want to see. You want to see that those things are bad and evil so you try to abolish them as much as possible. To sterilize yourself from evil is to *reject the truth*. But you can't reject evil, Michael, you just can't. It's impossible."

"Truth? What truth is there in saying that greed and envy, sickness and pain can have any place in life and that they can even be ... *good*?"

"You will have to figure that out for yourself, Michael. I can't tell you everything. Besides, you'll have plenty of time to figure that out, along with how to get off the electric chair—great invention, by the way. I know it's already been invented before, but I won't tell anyone. It'll be our little secret. I'll let you keep it from the outside if you promise to keep mine," Daniel said in a mocking way, knowing Michael wouldn't be able to stop him in time, and knowing how long it would take him to escape the electric chair, if at all.

"You won't tell me why you think sickness and greed are good things because you don't know *why* you think that. Whatever this hold is on you is distorting your mind. You're wrong, Father. Those are bad things, evil things."

"Oh, I'm not denying that they aren't wrong and evil, I'm saying they are necessary. But, call it what you will; I see what I have to do now and so does Amanda."

"You'll lose, Father. I know that, and you know that."

"Maybe, but little will the people know the real reason for all the evil and sickness that's going to spread throughout the New Earth once again is because of me, and the program that I have created. Once they drink from the Stream of Life, after thinking that when they do it will bring their loved ones back from the dead, in fact it will infect them, altering their genes and changing them from a peaceful and loving society into a society filled with greed, corruption, lies, and even murder. And those that follow me *will be gods* living on forever, just as I will. They will see a new world full of forgotten deep-rooted characteristics that make us truly HUMAN. The very essence of the *true* human spirit will be unleashed from within. No longer will the ways of the Old go unpracticed. We will have a new hierarchy for the New Earth. There will be power struggles, deceit, mistrust, and even murder...."

"That's twice now that you've mentioned murder, Father. Why do you have to kill people?"

But Daniel didn't hear his son's question and just continued with his speech. "... and they will be doing all this for that hope that they or their loved ones will get better. But I just know they will be doing it more for the chance of living forever by my side, as gods. And those that refuse to follow will be punished mightily; they will be hunted down and brought down to their knees, begging for mercy."

"God will never allow that, He will come back once he sees what you are doing."

"There *is* no God, Michael, none that I've seen. No, I've just seen a liar. We're just a charade, amusement, puppets. But I, Michael, shall no longer be *His* puppet. Not after He cut my strings, killing my wife and unborn son, and leaving me limp on the floor of his domain, forgotten."

"You're the one that's crazy, not me. I know this now. You still have a choice, though. Stop this now before you regret doing something you can't take back. Leave, I beg of you!"

"Beg? BEG? YOU *beg* of ME? No, my son, it's not I you should be begging for this to stop. I am going through with this, no matter what it takes. No, Michael, beg your precious 'God' to end this now. I know my role, and I have made peace with it. And what's the worst this 'God' of yours can do to me? I mean, I have already conquered death. Enough chat, though. I have lots of work to do, and very little time."

Michael struggled to escape again only to get shocked to the point of blacking out, having just enough strength to mutter, "Father! Father …. Why are you doing this to your only son? Why me?"

"Why, son—I thought it was obvious. Because you were the only one who could stop me."

Michael's head sank to his chest in defeat.
"Oh, Amanda, angel! It's time to go." She ran back in the room. "Amanda my angel, are you having fun inside this A.T.M.?"

"Oh, yes, Grandpa! What else can we do in here? I love A.T.M.s! I can't wait to get my very own!"

"I'm glad you asked, sweetheart; follow me and let's find out … and don't worry about Daddy, he's just spending some time here with the new invention he's working on: "the electric chair." He's testing it out right now, so let's not bother him. Now, let's go into a city, shall we?"

"Yay! Do I get to try more of my powers on the Sapiens-Old there, too?" she asked, thinking that she's still going to be inside the Machine of Forever, inside her Grandpa's heaven. She won't be practicing her new skills on the Sapiens-Old.

"You know it, angel, and anything your creative young mind can think of will come true. But, remember what we talked about, right? You won't be able to show your skills on the outside world, that's not possible to do for our kind just yet. Excuse me, *your* kind; I mean, after all, I've passed on."

"Yeah," she said despondently.

"Now, now, no more of that, it's only for a little while more. Remember you can practice ANYTHING you want in the privacy of Jacobs's house when we get there."

"He won't mind us staying there and me practicing my A.T.M. powers?"

"AMANDA!" Michael burst out, interrupting them after awakening again. "You're being tricked, baby! He is using you!"

"Oh, Daddy, you're so funny. He's just teaching me how to use my very own Atomic Transference Machine. I need all the practice I can get since my Big Bang is next week. With all this practicing, I can start my own civilizations sooner, though. Isn't that great?"

"That's right, Amanda, practice makes perfect. Jacob won't mind, I'm sure of it. And Daddy is just suffering from one of the effects of his newest invention. I suffered many times creating many things that you see and love and use today. He'll be fine, I promise."

"Amanda!" Michael struggled too hard; the electric current jolted through his entire system. Overloading his power intake, his nano-bots locked up. In self-defense, they started protecting his Vial of Viability; he screamed in pain from the locking of his nano-bots as they shut down in place, freezing him like a statue up to his neck. "Amanda, darling ... please help Daddy, I'm not testing a new invention at all. This is hurting, Daddy, help me…"

"Don't listen to him, angel, he doesn't know what he's saying. It's just another side effect from the invention of his, speaking in tongues." Daniel led his granddaughter through the thick stone doorway, out into the thicker jungle and looked back. "Enjoy testing your new invention, son. Don't worry about your darling little daughter, Michael. I'll make sure she's nice and safe with me. She has to be safe. After all, she has to usher in a divine new way of life for our race. I'll lay out the groundwork for her, making sure everyone will be at his or her weakest state of mind from the sickness, desperate for some sort of help. Any help will suffice, since your 'God' is completely absent. We'll leave them to wonder why they are sick, where their God is, and why some have been cured while others are still sick, making things just ripe for her to come along and pick them off at will."

"I'll stop you once the next person comes to the Building of Souls to visit you. When they see me trapped here in this chair and not you, they'll free me. And when that person does, I will hunt you down to put an end to this. If my God truly is absent, I will fight for Him. I'll get others to fight for Him, and together WE *WILL WIN.*"

"Well, good luck with that then, son." Daniel walked over to him and kissed his forehead. "Do try and relax for now. Try not to shock yourself too much by attempting to escape that electric chair, my boy. Remember, if you struggle too hard, it might kill you. Even though this feels like this is the end, it isn't. I'm sure we will meet again."

He heard Daniel tell the people if they follow him now they will live as gods, forever rich and forever young, never dying. They shouted in a feverous joy, and, chanting "Daniel" and Amanda" as the two walked off into the distance.

Then it grew silent.

Michael screamed out in disgust and fright knowing his daughter was being seduced by the temptations of Satan, and he felt helpless at not being able to stop his own father.

"Noooooooooooo!"

As Daniel and Amanda reached the edge of the jungle, he pointed out to Amanda the giant city Aeon that lay before them. "This looks just like Aeon, because it was modeled after it. You can practice all that I've taught you and more here; but remember, only when I say so."

"Oh, this is so exciting! I can't wait, Grandpa, I've never been inside an A.T.M. like this before. Usually I just come with Daddy and watch what he does at his job. But this, this is something altogether different, I could have never imagined it could be so *real*."

"It is quite something special, isn't it, Amanda? I've learned some new things since I've passed on. I will teach you some of them, and together we will teach the universe." She yelled out with glee, taking his hand, and as they walked out behind the last patch of trees and bushes, he turned around and waved his hand. Blue energy waves flowed around the whole jungle, turning it to stone. The Stream of Life spilled over the top and ran around the entire east side of the city.

A few people looked upon them with amazement, for they'd never seen Daniel outside the Building of Souls, and alive again. "Amanda, get rid of them. They're not important right now; they're just a program, remember?" The people's expressions changed from awe and curiosity to fright and fear as Amanda pointed her finger at them and flashed lightning bolts toward them. Instantly, they caught fire, then dissolved away into ashes. There was barely enough time for them to scream. "Good work, angel. And don't worry, my darling one, they're only human."

Definitions

ATOMIC TRANSFERENCE MACHINE (A.T.M.) - They are machines that can create an entire universe inside the Atomic Transference Machine Squared for Modiens to help evolve their own Homo sapiens by teaching them in the ways of the universe. The machines themselves are located inside the rooms of the buildings and uses individual atoms to reconstruct anything the Modien needs/desires. Shaped like an office desk, Modiens place their Sphere of Life into the slot & the A.T.M.'s load the universe.

ATOMIC TRANSFERENCE MACHINE SQUARED (A.T.M.S.) - They're the buildings where Modiens go to work every day to create their own universe filled with the inhabitants of Homo sapiens. They're located in the middle of cities next to the Building of Souls its shape changes monthly by design via Modiens that have entered into raffles held in the cities. Each Modien spends at least five minutes inside their universe.

BALL OF ESSENCE - Massive ball of energy made entirely of Passed On Modiens' Modien Essence Transmitter (M.E.T.'s), it's the final resting place for the deceased of the Modien society. Once the Modiens turn 800 their M.E.T. is inserted into the Machine of Forever and entered into the Ball of Essence. Its massive energy output helps power the society of the New Earth. The Ball of Essence itself is inside a sealed off room consisting of massive lead walls which protects the visitors & the outside world from the intense radiation.

BUILDING OF SOULS - These Immense buildings each hold a Machine of Forever & a Ball of Essence & are designed differently but all share a distinctive set of sapphire steps leading to the entrance in the shape of a crescent moon. They're guarded by a Sentinel of Souls which scans a visiting relatives' Modien Essence Transmitter (M.E.T.'s) located on the top of their Vial of Viability. The Sentinel's then allow the visiting Modien inside. If there's any disturbance the Sentinels have the capability to shoot the Halo of Ataraxia at a Modien; If they are not registered to that particular building, If they are not of age (18) & without a parent, or lie about who they're visiting.

ESSENCE ACCUMULATING CENTER (E.A.C.) - Where Modiens go to have their DNA extracted to reproduce, located throughout the cities.

MACHINE OF FOREVER - Created by Daniel they lie inside the Building of Souls & use the Ball of Essence to extract The Heavenly Coded (Memories of the deceased and their characteristics & looks) to build an environment for the visiting relatives to interact with their loved ones. The generated material CANNOT leave the Machine of Forever, once visitors leave their assigned rooms, the information (the ones that have Passed On) reverts back into the Ball of Essence.

MODIENS ESSENCE EXTRACTION DEVICE (M.E.E.D.) - An extracting device that removes the DNA from the Modiens that want to reproduce offspring. It penetrates into the Modiens body, via their own self-defense that's built in to avoid foreign objects that would harm them such as hail, or falling objects of a certain size. Once close enough to the M.E.T., it bonds itself with the unknown material to allow the DNA to be extracted from within the vial of Viability. Once it has DNA from the parent that wants a child, it supplies another Vial of Viability for the child's DNA to go inside, another M.E.T. & Nano-bots for them to create a child.

MODIEN ESSENCE TRANSMITTER(M.E.T.) - A green pyramid-shaped piece made from an unknown material created by God which allows the DNA inside the Vial of Viability to be read by the Nano-bots then uses that info to make the Modien what it is(i.e. characteristics & features). Without this piece which is placed over the only opening inside the Vial of Viability, the Nano-bots are unable to read the DNA inside & no Modien is made. Only God can create these M.E.T.'s and shares the information on how to make them with only his closest friends.

SENTINEL OF SOULS - Protects the entrance to the Building of Souls and any teleports throughout the solar system. Sentinel of Souls scans the visiting relatives Modien Essence Transmitter (M.E.T.'s) located on the top of their Vial of Viability. The Sentinel's then allow the visiting Modien inside. If there's any disturbance the Sentinels have the capability to shoot the Halo of Ataraxia at a Modien; If they are not registered to that particular building, If they are not of age (18), or lie about who they're visiting.

SPHERE OF LIFE - A purple, marble-sized ball that sits on top of the Modien Essence Transmitter that collects, records, and stores all the planets/civilizations a Modien has worked on throughout their time in the A.T.M./universe. It only works only inside the rooms of the Machine of Forever & can only work when it's combined with The Heavenly Integument of Space to create entire universes for Modiens to work inside.

STREAM OF LIFE - The program that Daniel designs to escape the Machine of Forever, it links his heaven to the outside world.

THE HIGH COALITION OF SPACE-TRAVELING BEINGS (T.H.C.S.B.) - A committee of all space-traveling beings that govern the universe, Modiens are chosen to become diplomats in the T.H.C.S.B. only if they have original members of The Old as family.

THE POTHER OF SATAN – A luminescent mist that is Satan himself, and after his powers was stripped he was humiliated and shape-shifted into The Pother. If a Modien looks too long at it they see their favorite thing in the universe and want to get it. Looking too long allows Satan to escape the cage and enter the Modien conscious to start spreading evil again by altering their DNA to generate more of the evil side of their genes causing The Sickness (i.e. greed, sickness, jealousy, selfishness).

THE HEAVENLY CODED - The final program written by individual Modiens based on their life experiences, their looks & characteristics. The lives of Modiens are constantly being recording and on their Modien Essence Transmitter which is put into the Ball of Essence upon their death. The Machine of Forever reads The Heavenly Coded and recreates that information for visitors when they come to be with their loved ones that's Passed On.

THE HEAVENLY INTEGUMENT OF SPACE (T.H.I.S.) - Substance given to the Modiens by God to coat the outside of the rooms of the A.T.M.'s which creates the empty space needed for the many universes created by Modiens. T.H.I.S. is also used by the Modiens homes, where their apartments in the skyscrapers so they can have a good sized piece of land that can extend inside the home but doesn't take up space with the adjoining apartments. The colliding integuments create power for the Modien society.

THE SICKNESS - The symptoms Modiens get when they drink from the Stream Of Life, once Modiens drink from the Stream Of Life it alters their DNA by activating the weaker side of the genes(i.e. love/hate, greed/selflessness, happiness/envy) to produce them more, activating the sides of(hate, greed, envy) the genes making them the more prominent producer inside the genes. No one has drunk from it, only Daniel.

VIAL OF VIABILITY - The container that holds the DNA strands of Modiens that sits inside Modiens where the Homo sapiens heart are. They're made from the strongest elements in the universe to protect the valuable DNA inside. The parents (when they turn 200) are able to have children of their own & they can choose their children's looks, and the traits that they will accede in i.e. interests in a particular science & or literature & arts, to even how much charisma they have and if they are good in sports. Modiens love to learn and always try to improve themselves so if they lack a certain trait and realize it, they want to obtain that skill they're lacking to make them a better being. Without that DNA inside the Vial of Viability, Modiens would fall apart, not having the instructions telling their Nano-bots how to assemble themselves into looking and feeling like a Homo-sapiens.

DEDICATIONS

I'd first like to dedicate this to my mother Elaine, my wonderful editor Laura, my exceptionally talented artist Andrianna, friends that's supported me throughout my writing and trying to get it completed; The sweetest woman Kristie Lake, my buddy Allison(P3) & Angie Bazzle, Allen my mentor, Marilyn, Amanda(all), Joey, Ray, Becki, The Flying Wo-Lynda, Gina, Sabrina, Ginger, The Skipper, Mary Jane, Shake, Angel, Crystal, Paul, Wayne, Susan, Nikki(all), Robert's, Brady. Aimie,

Douglas, Christy, and Michael(all) My incredible sisters, they know who they are...
well okay Zandessa and Alyson!! Anyone else I missed love you guys!!

ABOUT MYSELF

Born in California, and a little stop at Denver, I'm just a shy guy with big dreams
and lots of hope. I grew up just outside of Philly and had a decent life. I've had a
mixed life filled with ups and downs like everyone else, only I had a vision of this
story so I went with it and here we are. I'm in sunny Florida and enjoying my life
now all thanks to my imagination that has never let me done, and I hope it doesn't
let you down. Enjoy, there's more to come.

www.ingramcontent.com/pod-product-compliance
Lightning Source LLC
Chambersburg PA
CBHW070853120626
46556CB00002B/974